CU01080779

TRAVELLING LIGHT
LEGENDS OF AN INDIAN FAKIR

Encounters with people good and bad, wild animals, ogres, devils
and deities

WITH ILLUSTRATIONS FOR COLOURING
BY GEETANJALI KAPOOR

The author will donate all royalties from this book to Flora & Fauna
International (FFI) for wildlife protection in Africa.

Retold by
Naginder Sehmi

TRAVELLING LIGHT
LEGENDS OF AN INDIAN
FAKIR

Vanguard Press

VANGUARD PAPERBACK

© Copyright 2020
Naginder Sehmi
Illustrated by Geetanjali Kapoor

The right of Naginder Sehmi
to be identified as author of
this work has been asserted by him in accordance with the
Copyright, Designs and Patents Act 1988.

All Rights Reserved

No reproduction, copy or transmission of this publication
may be made without written permission.
No paragraph of this publication may be reproduced,
copied or transmitted save with the written permission of the publisher, or in
accordance with the provisions
of the Copyright Act 1956 (as amended).

Any person who commits any unauthorised act in relation to
this publication may be liable to criminal
prosecution and civil claims for damages.

A CIP catalogue record for this title is
available from the British Library.

ISBN 978 1 78465 804 5

Vanguard Press is an imprint of
Pegasus Elliot MacKenzie Publishers Ltd.
www.pegasuspublishers.com

First Published in 2020

Vanguard Press
Sheraton House Castle Park
Cambridge England

Printed & Bound in Great Britain

Dedication

Dedicated to all those people who desire to save the earth from human greed.

Contents

BACKGROUND

Introduction

Reflecting on my "why" on writing this book stirred up strong thoughts. When children read stories from around the world, they learn new perspectives that both extend beyond and above their own context and subsequently allow them to connect with other diverse contexts. Stories are a fundamental means of how we pass on history and cultural empathy to children.

I kept the image of my Uncle Santa with me as I retold these tales. He was a remarkable storyteller and village musician gifted for narrating the adventures of Baba Nanak. We would all sit on the floor and Santa with his lengthy silvery beard and strident voice and smiling all the while would take us on a journey along with Baba Nanak, where we would meet demons, magicians, cannibal-kings, magician-queens, thieves, and malefactors of all kinds.

My wish is that these stories captivate the minds of today's children in the same way I myself had been enchanted. Relax, sit back, enjoy and indulge your inner child as you read these stories to your own children.

Power of myths

The extraordinary travel tales of Nanak Dev written in the sixteenth century follow the world's ancient tradition of telling mythological tales as heroic travel yarns. In the Hindu epic *Ramayana*, Prince Rama was condemned and banished for fourteen years into the wilderness. Angels and devils actively participated in his innumerable incredible adventures; even an army of flying monkeys helped to finally save him and his wife from a demon king. For many years *Ramayana* television serials have determined the daily timetable of the entire Indian people. One cannot even dare to estimate the force of the impact of these tales on human spiritual psyche. Rama is worshipped as a God by millions today.

In Europe, for many centuries, Homer's *Odyssey* of the Greek voyager-hero Ulysses has played a similar role. The roots of Judaic faiths are traced back to the miraculous episodes during the Exodus led by Moses. The great Norse myths, with their travel-tales of dwarfs, glacial giants, gods, and a great deal of magic, have had a strong impact on European thought. In recent times we know of *Sindbad the Sailor* and *Gulliver's Travels*. We continue to emulate them in episodes of *Star Wars* and numerous other galactic journeys. People endowed with rich imagination, philosophic vision, or spiritual thoughts have often used travel stories as a means of portraying their ideas, especially to engage young minds and people who are illiterate.

Evidently, travel sagas form an ideal medium to bring together and convey to the public miscellaneous remembrances, scattered folklore and reflective thoughts. The impact of travel-tale-telling on the mindset of people, especially the young, and on human history is often overlooked.

The extraordinary travel tales of Baba Nanak are probably among the last of such traditional writings, partly historical and partly conjectural. It is not surprising that it is the conjectural, miraculous aspect that has swayed the Sikh psyche deeply, transforming Nanak into God when Sikhs know very well that this is diametrically opposed to the message in his writings. "It's all Baba Nanak's blessing," with hands folded said the Sikh owner of a flourishing sports shop in a country town. Poor God has been supplanted by a mythical Nanak. Today, learned people find it impossible to undo the negative impact of these tales.

Nanak could not escape the human craving for telling imaginary tales. Many years after Nanak died, some story tellers used his real travel route as a string and beaded it with scrambled memories of Nanak's life, embellishing them with folkloric fables and miracles. They quite succeeded in creating a Sikh mythology.

Nanak and the traveller's tales

Nanak Dev is best known from the tales in the four *Janamsakhis* (accounts of birth and life), which were set down a century after his death. With his companions Bala the Hindu, and Mardana the Muslim, Nanak travelled for twenty-four years in regions of what are now India, Arabia, Iraq, Iran, Afghanistan, Tibet, and Sri Lanka. No other prophet had ever travelled so far. Thanks to his tales, historians have been able to reconstruct the routes followed by Nanak Dev, discover the places he visited, and confirm the dates as well.

Who was Baba Nanak?

Few people are familiar with Nanak Dev the reformer, legendary voyager and incomparable poet. He was born on April 15, 1469—although his birthday is now celebrated in November—in the small village of Talvandi, near the great city of Lahore in what was then India. At that time Pakistan did not exist.

Thanks to the surprising intellectual, emotional and spiritual intelligence and affability he showed since childhood, he achieved great works in literary, social, philosophical, and religious areas. It is said that his guru was nature itself. His lively mind observed everything around him, accumulating an incredible store of knowledge during his long journeys.

Over the course of his life he fought tirelessly against bad religious and social practices in order to elevate human dignity. It was his ambition to expand and put into action the idea of the brotherhood of mankind, an egalitarian society without distinctions of caste or religion, as well as the equality of men and women.

At the end of his last journey, Nanak built the village of Kartapur (Creator's City) on the right bank of the Ravi River. Here he lived the rest of his life. He gathered many disciples around his innovative and modern ideas. One of these disciples, Lehna, was chosen by Nanak to be his successor. Nanak gave him a new name, Angad, which means "part of my own body and of myself." Nanak Dev died on September 22, 1539 at the age of seventy.

His writings

Nanak was an admirable poet. He translated his thoughts in the form of poetry, mainly during his travels, and would sing his songs whenever the occasion presented itself. This work was the first literary masterpiece in the Punjabi language. To become more familiar with Nanak Dev one must study and understand his poems, which are juxtaposed with the compositions of other writers and arranged according to musical chords,

Raag (Raga), in the Sikh sacred book called *Sri Guru Granth Sahib Ji* (*Adi Granth*).

It is the depth of his thoughts that makes Nanak a true guru. His poems are of inestimable value on a literary, linguistic and philosophical level; most of the time they are made even more glorious by their musical elegance. Many different peoples, Sikhs in particular, sing these poems as prayers.

Nanak Dev is called "Baba" out of respect for a mature and wise person. In the stories of his adventures he is often called *Fakir*. Even today people remember him in a couplet:

Nanak, shah fakir,

Hindu ka guru Musulman ka pir

(Nanak, shah fakir; guru of the Hindus and guide of the Moslems)

These stories are intended above all for young people. For parents, these tales, rich in extraordinary and humorous anecdotes, are perfect for telling at bedtime. My own hero is Mardana, because he is funny and entertaining and always finds his way into trouble. I was captivated and fascinated by the miraculous ways in which Baba Nanak always managed to rescue him.

Role of the tales

As in most religious gatherings, the narrator-musician uses these tales to instruct and to reinforce the image of Nanak Dev by associating the stories with specific poems from the Sikh sacred scripture, the *Adi Granth*. Using these anecdotes, the narrator makes the culminating point of the moral in epigraph form. In that sense, these are also pedagogical tools par excellence. However, it is difficult, if not impossible, to confirm the veracity of numerous "miraculous" acts that Nanak is said to have performed in the course of his extraordinary travels. For those who believe the stories as told in images, the miracles are doubtlessly true.

Was Nanak a magician, and did he perform miracles?

In the tales, Nanak performs numerous miracles. These episodes are fictitious; Nanak Dev was fiercely opposed to the idea of miracles and magic. The tales contain a great many chronological inconsistencies and miraculous elements that involve magic and false belief, plundering and perverting ideas from his poems. Nanak was a great and courageous person who undertook long and perilous voyages. He encountered all kinds of people, good and bad.

In order to set people on the right path, he would often create a funny situation. For Nanak Dev nature itself was a miracle. It was not divine intervention that saved the three travellers from injuries and mishaps. It was the "magic" of Nanak's words. He had a way of speaking that caught the adversary, the enemy, or the challenger in a web of dialogue from which they could not shake loose. Such was the power of his words.

In the era when these stories were written, faith and belief were much more important than knowledge. Few could explain Nanak's ideas of innovation to illiterate people. A significant segment of society earned its living by exploiting ignorant people through false religious practices. These tales, put together for the most part by people who were close to Nanak Dev's family but who had ill intentions, succeeded in swaying the entire Sikh community and even separating them from the teachings of Nanak. This was a subtle and successful course used by traditionalist Hindus to pollute Nanak's writings by associating his poems with ancient Indian myths involving gods and goddesses. Several of the stories make no sense, have no logic or utility, and are chronologically impossible. With the addition of traditional images to the recounting of miracles, the stories have become a powerful but false belief. They often insult Nanak's humanity and transform him into an extraordinary superhuman figure—something Nanak Dev would never have wanted.

His songs

By reading his songs http://bigbangyoga.org/les-chants-de-nanak-dev/ (also available as Kindle edition, Amazon - https://www.amazon.com/Chansons-Nanak-Dev-French-ebook/dp/B07NGMSGXR) we find that Nanak is not a saint, nor a yogi or bhakta, nor a reformer of religion such as Martin Luther, nor an avatar come down from heaven, nor a *rishi*, nor a prophet sent by God. In some ways he is all, but really, he is a guru or a perfect master who, with his 974 songs, tried hard in a new way to dispel the darkness of thought and remove the veil of ignorance of human beings and in this way redress the corrupt society.

Sources of the tales

The tales have been drawn from the four *Janamsakhis*. They differ significantly in terms of both chronology and detail:

Puratan Janamsakhi (Valayatwali Janamsakhi) Sri Guru Nanak Dev Ji. Ca. 1634. Edited by Bhai Vir Singh.

Bhai Bala Janamsakhi: 1658.

Janamsakhi Miharban: Manohar Das Miharban (1581-1640).

Bhai Mani Singh Janamsakhi: End of the 17th century.

In the present collection the retold tales follow the chronological sequence of stories adopted by Dr. Kirpal Singh in the following two works:

Janamsakhi Tradition—An Analytical Study. Dr. Kirpal Singh, 2004, Singh Brothers, Amritsar.

Atlas, Travels of Guru Nanak. Fauja Singh and Kirpal Singh, Punjabi University, Patiala, 1976.

The following works have served as valuable references:

Stories from Sikh History—Book 1. Kartar Singh and Gurdial Singh Dhillon, Hemkunt Press, New Delhi, 1971.

Sri Narankari Chamatkar. Giani Singh, Bh. Chatar Singh Jeevan Singh, Amritsar, 2013.

Travels of Guru Nanak. Surinder Singh Kohli, Publication Bureau, Panjab University, Chandigarh.

Guru Nanak, le Messager de l'Unité. Gérard Bossy, Edition L'Or du temps, 1991.

Les Sikhs. Michel Delahoutre, Édition Brepols, 1989.

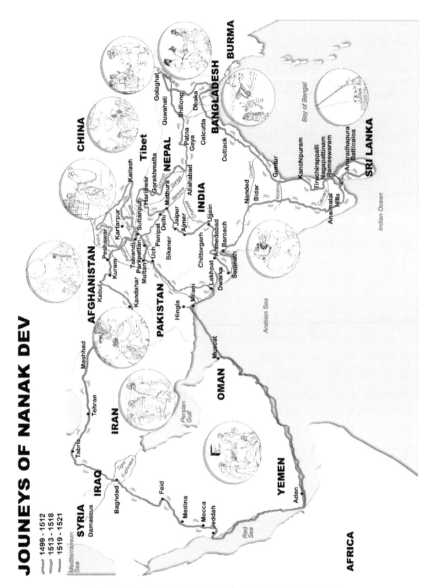

MAP OF NANAK'S TRAVELS

1. A NEW SHINING STAR

Nanak Dev? That's not an English name. Certainly not. It was 1469, the fifteenth day of April. An hour past midnight the bright moon lit up the countryside. Spring was on full display. The golden wheat fields were ready to be harvested. The peacock strutted and fanned the magnificent colours of his feathers. Countless birds in the green trees chirped happily. The branches of the mango trees curved with the weight of juicy yellow fruit.

I'm telling you about the country of Punjab, in northern India. At that time Pakistan did not exist. The pundit, the village fortune teller, had foretold the coming of Nanak Dev. He announced, "A star has descended from the sky to bring desperately needed light that will transform the world." A pundit is a learned man usually belonging to the highest Hindu caste of Brahmins. Besides being a fortune teller, he can be a priest, teacher, medicine man and advisor.

Heavenly music resounded in God's palace. Thirty-three million gods and goddesses, as well as yogis and monks, knelt before the new-born. The entire world danced joyously and sang the celestial song of peace.

The newly born would rekindle the light in these dark times. At that time India was decadent; this child was going to lift the fog of ignorance, sin, corruption and superstition and replace them with love. When he was a little older, he wrote a poem about it.

This age is like a sharp knife; the kings are like butchers.
Goodness has taken wing and flown away;
In the dark night of falsehood.
I spy not the moon of truth anywhere.
I grope after truth and am bewildered.
Sin is king, and greed the minister,
And falsehood is the chief agent;
Lust is their constant adviser;
The people are ignorant and sworn to sloth;
Priests dance, play music and masquerade;
They scream and howl as they sing odes;
The ignorant pretend to be knowledgeable,
And deceptive argument passes for wisdom;

Those who do noble acts gain nothing;
Their only hope is to gain salvation in return.

Mothers and fathers with their children, the young and the old, came to express their good wishes to Nanak's mother, Tripta, and his father, Kalu Mehta Kalyan of the Kshatriya caste.

Nanak was born in Talvandi, a modest village now called Nankana Sahib, near Lahore in Pakistan. His mother soon noticed that her son was different from other children. He did not cry and charmed everyone with his beautiful eyes and smile. His father Kalu was a loyal accountant for the district chief, Rai Bular, a Muslim. Nanak had a sister Nanki who was five years older. She was the first to notice that her brother radiated a godly light. Rai Bular was a generous person who made no distinction between Hindus and Muslims. He loved baby Nanak.

2. MARDANA DOES NOT DIE

Nanak was a happy child. At the age of five he would listen attentively when people spoke with each other. People would come to listen to him talk about logic, or infinity. Hindus saw him as an avatar of God, and Muslims claimed that he was Allah's prophet. He would often spend hours in contemplation instead of playing with other children. Sometimes, Nanak and his friends would tenderly sing hymns. He shared what he had with his playmates. Everyone loved him. He would ask his mother for food, clothes and money to give to the poor.

Very active and athletic, he loved playing hide-and-seek and other games. He could run faster than most other children. In some ways they considered him their leader. He often brought them home and asked his kindly mother to give them sweets. One of Nanak's best friends was a Muslim boy whose parents belonged to the caste of musicians. One day while looking for him, Nanak saw a grieving crowd gathered in front of his friend's house. He saw his friend lying under a white sheet in the middle of the courtyard.

Nanak said, "What are you doing hiding here? Get up! Let's go!"

"He is dead," said someone sadly.

"Mardana—not dead," said Nanak. "Come on, let's play." Nanak pulled on the sheet. The boy opened his eyes, got up and walked away with Nanak.

Completely dumbfounded, the people who had gathered could not believe their eyes. This was how the boy got the name Mardana.

Endnote: Nanak's friend had already been given the name Mardana, which means "Like a man, strong and brave." The word meaning "not dead" was made up for the story. Mardana, who was born in Talvandi in 1459, was ten years older than Nanak.

3. NANAK GOES TO SCHOOL

When Nanak was seven, his father said, "You are a big boy. Now should go to school." Kalu took him to the village school and asked the teacher, Gopal, to educate him. Gopal wrote on a patti, a wooden tablet, the Sanskrit alphabet containing thirty-five letters. "Now you read these," he told the young boy. Instead of reading the letters, Nanak composed a poem of thirty-five couplets, one for each letter.

On the second day of school, Nanak remained silent. The teacher asked, "Why aren't you reading today?"

"Master, do you have enough knowledge to teach me?"

"Of course. I have read all that exists: the Vedas and other ancient scriptures, as well as accountancy and astrology!"

Nanak responded, "Studying too much can suffocate us; it's a waste of time." Then he sang the first couplet of his poem:

Throw your worldly love into the fire, then grind it to make ink.
With your intelligence make paper of purest quality.
Make of your love a pen and make your mind a scribe.
Seek advice from the Master and write down your thoughts.

Nanak continued, "If you own all this knowledge, pass it also to me. But listen: Wherever your soul would go, this knowledge will be your calling card. The angel of death will never torment you."

"Who has taught you all this?" Gopal inquired. "Nanak, tell me why we should pray."

"We pray to be always happy," Nanak replied.

The teacher was surprised and amazed by this young student, who was speaking subtle truths about human beings and God.

Then Nanak asked his teacher, "Teach me only letters that define God and tell me about his marvellous creation. Without knowing God and the gate that leads to his service, all knowledge is useless."

"But listen, Nanak—those who pray do not have enough to eat. They are ignored by all. But those who are rich and who govern do many bad things; they are not afraid of anybody, even God."

"In the afterlife, they will be punished, beaten the way the laundry man beats clothes, ground like mustard grains in the grinding mill, and chained in hell," young Nanak replied.

Nanak's words reflected such peaceful ardour that Gopal knelt before him and said, "You are my teacher and I am your student."

From that point on Nanak stopped going to school.

Endnote: At school Nanak studied diligently and learned quickly. The poems he is supposed to have composed in this story were actually written when Nanak was an adult.

4. THE RITUAL OF THE SACRED THREAD (JANEU)

When Nanak was nine, his parents held the ceremony of Yajnopavit. This is a ceremony of putting on the child a sacred thread called a janeu. The pundit Hardyal, the Hindu priest, came with a janeu made of cotton. The ground reserved for the ceremony was purified by coating it with cow dung mixed with mud. Nanak was made to sit there, and the pundit whispered in his ear, "You're a Kshatriya. Our religion requires you to wear a janeu."

When the pundit raised the cord to put around his head, Nanak held Hardyal's hand and stopped him. That astonished the people who had gathered. Many tried to convince the boy to follow the tradition. But Nanak said with a smile, "What a strange ceremony! The Brahmin spins the cotton into a cord and he never separates it from his body. When the cord is used up, he replaces it. If the cord were magical, it would never break. Have you a cord that can control your perceptions of your five senses?"

The priest panicked and quickly asked for his fees for performing the ceremony. But Nanak addressed the gathering, "This priest is proud of having the power to tell the future. His arrogance limits his actions, and now he is seriously trying to show the merits of a sacred cord, putting it around the necks of others. This man pretends to be enlightened, but he is blind."

He told Hardyal, "I will not wear this cord, which is no more sacred than the cotton it's made of."

The embarrassed priest then asked him, "What sort of cord do you want to wear?" And Nanak replied:

Make the cord from the cotton of compassion, spun with contentment;
Tie it with the knot of chastity;

Give it the twists of virtues.
If you have such a cord, O Brahmin, put it around my neck;
Once put on, it will never tear or soil, neither burn nor become lost.
Blessed is the person who wears such a cord.

Nanak's words touched the hearts of the people who had gathered, and the ceremony was stopped.

Endnote: Nanak did not recite these verses during the ceremony but many years later.

5. BETROTHAL AND MARRIAGE

Kalu was sitting in front of the house when his son and the boy's teacher Gopal approached him. He immediately assumed that the boy had done something wrong. He was ready to punish him. But Gopal inter- posed. "Kalu, your son is not an ordinary boy. I'm convinced that he is the incarnation of God."

Kalu replied angrily, "Why are you praising this boy? I simply want him to be sufficiently educated so that he can earn his living well."

The teacher replied, "Educate him? But he knows everything. I showed him the importance of keeping accounts and juggling with numbers. But this amazing boy already knows them all. How can I continue teaching him?"

Before leaving he said, "His knowledge of life surpasses mine. Believe me, he is destined to save the world."

Kalu remained silent but unconvinced. He saw his son as hard-headed, obstinate, passing his time doing nothing, or daydreaming or sleeping. "You are already nine. If you continue like this, what will become of you? What will you live on?"

One day Kalu tapped lovingly on his son's shoulder and said, "Go to the madrassa, the Islamic school, and learn Farsi, the official language here."

He went to the madrassa and was thoroughly bored because he spoke Farsi well already. He did not talk to anybody.

Then the villagers advised Kalu, "You should marry him off."

In those days, children were married very young. Kalu followed the villagers' advice. He called in the family priest and asked him to find a suitable girl for Nanak. In his search he reached Pakhoke Randhawe, a village on the east bank of the River Ravi about thirty kilometers away. There lived a man named Moolla. He was the village patwari (tax collector and record keeper). He was also of the same Kshatriya caste. He offered to marry his daughter, Ghummi, to Nanak. Thus, Nanak was married at the age of nine. After the marriage, in accordance with tradition, the girl's name was changed to Sulakhani. She came to live with Nanak seven years later.

6. FIELD GREEN AGAIN

Like all parents, Kalu wanted his son to have a comfortable life. He saw that Nanak preferred to pass his days in the countryside feeling free in nature. He loved feeding cows and buffalo and considered them to be his companions. One day Kalu suggested to him, "Why don't you take the cattle to graze?"

"I would love it!" Nanak replied.

Every morning Nanak took the cattle to graze in the green meadow, and in the evening, he brought them to the farmhouse to be milked. The cattle also liked being with him.

Often, he would sit in the cool shade of a banyan tree, an Indian variety of the fig tree. He passed long hours listening to the sounds of nature and looking at the blue sky. One afternoon when it was very hot, our young herdsman dozed in the shade of a tree. The cattle, grazing calmly, moved away to the middle of a wheat field, beautifully golden and ready to be harvested. The field belonged to a neighbour named Bhatti. Nanak suddenly woke up, startled by Bhatti's screams.

"I'm ruined! Get up, you sloth! See what your cattle have done. All my wheat has been plundered," he shouted angrily.

Nanak looked at him with candour and said, "Nothing is destroyed. The cattle have eaten just a little bit. All is God's gift; my grass is your grass. Calm down and be patient. All that these poor creatures of God have eaten will be returned to you a hundredfold, because God is generous."

But Bhatti, furious, did not see it that way. The two of them went to see Rai Bular, the village chief. The farmer told his story and moaned.

"You calm down," the chief consoled him. "This boy is a dreamer. Someone, go look for his father," Rai Bular ordered.

Kalu turned up as soon as he could.

"Why haven't you educated your son properly?" the chief asked. "He has not learned how to take care of his cattle. Now, this man's crop has been damaged. You must pay to compensate the loss; otherwise you will be summoned before the governor."

Kalu replied, "What could I do? In spite of all my efforts this boy does not want to change and continues to be irresponsible."

"In that case, I declare you guilty and you must pay back Bhatti."

At that moment Nanak spoke out, "Oh honourable chief, your decision will be executed if you find that even one ear of wheat crop is missing. I request that you send your officers and check."

Rai Bular proposed, "Go there together and evaluate the damage. I myself will ensure that Kalu pays for the loss of your crop."

When the group reached the field... what a surprise! Instead of a ravaged field, they saw the field full of lovely wheat ears filled with golden grain. They could not believe their eyes; a miracle had just occurred. The officer in charge reported everything to the chief, who declared, "Nothing is owed to Bhatti, and Nanak can go home with his father."

Before they parted, Rai Bular told Kalu, "Our Nanak loves God. He thinks of him all the time. God showed his love by restoring the ravaged crop as if nothing had happened. Be gentle with him. If he gives you trouble, I'll take care of it."

Endnote: We noted earlier that Nanak was very intelligent, strong, active, and conscientious. But according to this story he was lazy. Had God helped Nanak by restoring the wheat crop to reward a lazy boy? Actually, Nanak belonged to an upper caste and could not have been a herdsman.

7. COBRA AND SHADE

To most people, Nanak seemed to be living in a different world. He was often solemn and pensive. No one could help him out of this state. But that did not stop him from continuing to work as a herdsman.

One day, the chief of the village witnessed a strange episode. As he returned to his village, he saw Nanak lying motionless in the field. At his side an enormous cobra deployed his wide hood as if protecting the sleeper's head from the hot sun. The chief immediately assumed that the venomous serpent had bitten the boy and that he was dead. He quickly approached the boy. What happened then was astonishing: the cobra caught sight of the chief, folded its umbrella-like hood, and discreetly disappeared. Nanak woke up and saluted Rai Bular with a charming smile. The chief jumped down from his horse and held Nanak in his arms.

Another time, Rai Bular was returning from a hunting expedition. He saw Nanak's cattle grazing calmly in the meadow. He looked for Nanak everywhere but could not find him. It was very hot, and the shadows of all the trees had slowly moved, except for that of one tree. Under it, Nanak was asleep. The shade had stopped for Nanak. From that day the village chief was convinced that Nanak was divine.

8. EARNING A LIVING

Nanak continued to look after the cattle herd. He was often seen conversing with monks, bards and fakirs but talked little with others. His strange behaviour worried his family. They began to believe that Nanak had lost his head. One day his mother Tripta decided to talk to him. "My son, you know that spending all your time with fakirs will not help. You have a family. How are you going to feed them? In any case you must earn your living. Stop behaving like this. The whole village is making fun of us because our lazy son will do anything not to work."

This talk greatly saddened poor Nanak. Not knowing what to do, he lay down and four days passed.

His wife, Sulakhani, much disturbed, complained to her mother-in-law, "How can you just sit while your son is lying there? He has not eaten for four days."

Tripta got up, went to Nanak, and said, "My son, lying down like this has no meaning. Eat and drink a little. Go and check our fields. Think of feeding the family. Look for a job. The entire family is worried about you."

She continued, "If that does not suit you, then do nothing. We will no longer insist. But tell me, what is bothering you?"

When Kalu learned about Nanak, he was much disturbed. He was a man of action and wanted to call his son out, but his wife calmed him down.

Kalu spoke to Nanak, "I know you are not doing your work. You make me feel ashamed. People of Kshatriya caste must possess certain wealth. It is important that a man earn his living. In any case, if this work does not interest you, then you should become a peasant. Our family owns one neglected piece of land that needs to be prepared for cultivation. I'm sure any crop will grow well there. Then everyone will say, 'How nice Kalu's son is!'"

Nanak reacted, "Oh, Father, I'm already busy with another kind of cultivation—the real one. I've ploughed the soil, sowed the seeds, fenced the field, and I keep watch all the time. If I'm not capable of looking after my own crop, how can I take care of others?"

Exasperated, Kalu asked, "What cultivation are you talking about? You've never ploughed the field! Stop speaking like an imbecile! If you had worked as you say, you would be feeding your family!"

"I've prepared the soil, and the wheat is growing well."

"What are you trying to tell me?"

"You do not see it, but listen to what I'm going to recite:
Make your body the field and your mind the ploughman, your good action—cultivation;
Turn your work and your strength into water, make your body the field.
Sprinkle the seed of Name, make your feeling of contentment the leveller,
And living simply your field fence.
With your love and His grace, the seed will germinate, and you will see your mind enriched."

Refusing to listen to his son any further, Kalu said, "If you don't like agriculture, why don't you open a shop? Commerce is, in fact, the occupation of our caste." Then Nanak replied with a second verse

Make your life the space in the shop;
Make the eternal Name your merchandise;
Make concentration and reason your warehouse and store the Name in it;
In trading the Name with such merchants, the profit will be a mind filled with joy.

But Kalu did not take the young man's wise words seriously. He continued to insist and pushed his son to find useful and gainful work. "If running a shop does not attract you, become a horse trader. This will enable you to discover new countries."

Then Nanak sang a third verse:

Make trading in horses your listening to scripture reading;
Adopt irreproachable behaviour for advancing;
Make collecting of good deeds; your travelling expenses;
O mind, don't leave all this for tomorrow;
When you reach the country of Formless, you'll find the place of
happiness.

Tired, Kalu finally advised his son, "You can work for the government. I have friends and I can arrange to find you a good job."

To this Nanak replied, "I am already employed in the service of my Master, and you too should serve him." then he started to sing:

Concentrate on your job of guarding the Name in your mind;
Apply your efforts, renounce vices; thus, all will praise you;
Seeing you work in this way, His grace will glorify you fourfold.

Kalu felt that he was losing his son. In the village, rumours began to circulate. People said that Kalu's son had gone mad, that he had lost his mind.

9. A GOOD BARGAIN

Kalu saw his son as headstrong and lazy, wasting his time in useless meditations. One day he went to see him. Gently touching his shoulder, he spoke to him tenderly. "My son, you are now sixteen years old. It's time that you learn to engage in honest and profitable business. Here, take twenty rupees." In those times this was a great amount of money! "Go to the city of Chuharkana three or four hours' walk from here. Take your friend Bala with you. Today there is a big market there. Buy goods at a low price and then sell them at a higher price. In this way you will make a profit. Will that please you?"

Nanak agreed, took the money, and along with Bala set out on the road to the city. On the way he saw a group of hermits resting under a tree. Nanak was attracted to them and he joined the group. Talking to them, he learned that they had not eaten for many days. He felt very bad.

As Bala was becoming impatient, they got back on the road. In the market they bought a lot of foodstuffs. On the return journey, Nanak walked straight to the hungry hermits and distributed all the food. Bala watched, absolutely bewildered.

"Your father didn't give you money for this. He will be very angry."

The two young men continued their journey without saying a word. When they approached their village, Nanak stopped near a big tree and asked his friend to return alone. The branches of this tree touched the ground all around and formed a cosy shelter. Knowing that his father, who loved money, would be annoyed to find out what happened to the money he'd given his son, Nanak decided to spend the night in this shelter.

When Bala came to Nanak's house, Kalu was surprised to see Bala alone. Bala nervously told the story of the day's events.

"Take me to him!" Kalu ordered.

He found Nanak calmly sitting under the tree in contemplation. His father grabbed him roughly.

"What are you doing here? Where is the money I entrusted you with?"

The young man opened his eyes and looked at his father tenderly but without answering.

Kalu caught his arm and forcibly brought him out of the shelter. He slapped him and said, "You have wasted my money!"

Nanak took the punishment calmly. The noise attracted Nanak's sister and other villagers. The young girl stood between the two and saved her brother. That stirred up Kalu's anger even more, and he wanted to hit Nanak again. But he stopped when he saw Rai Bular, the village chief, coming. All saluted the chief with respect and, as expected, he demanded to know what was happening. After listening to Kalu and Bala, he turned to Nanak. "Why have you acted like this?"

"My father asked me to make a fair trade. By feeding the poor hungry people, I thought I could not have made a greater profit," Nanak replied calmly.

Rai Bular, who was very discerning, said to the irritated father, "Your son is destined not to deal in worldly goods but to profit from paradise. Don't be angry with him. Leave him to follow his own way because this is the best for all of us."

10. NANAK FALLS SICK

Three months passed. Nanak did not eat or drink much. Everyone thought that he had caught some strange disease and was mentally unsound. Some said that a bad spirit had overpowered him. In vain, many tried to help him out of his muteness. Some advised Kalu, "Why do you just sit and do nothing to help your son? Try to find a good Ayurvedic doctor who can give him good medicine. Your son is good and will make you proud."

Kalu and his wife decided to call on Hari Das, the village doctor. "How is Nanak?" the doctor asked.

Tripta replied, "Nanak has always preferred to be alone. He avoids company and spends hours in silence. Sometimes he disappears into nature for days without caring about anything; he seems to be losing himself in silence."

Kalu added, "He talks about strange things. He claims that his heart senses the pleading cries of millions of souls crushed by the weight of their sins. He wants to save the unfortunate of the world. He is disappointed by life. Do you think you can treat him?"

Tripta continued, "What breaks my heart is when I see him sobbing with anxiety. He has lost much weight. I think he has some illness. He tries to hide his suffering."

Hari Das accompanied them back home. He held Nanak's arm to take his pulse. But Nanak pulled it back and recited a verse in a voice full of tenderness:

They have called you so that you can treat my illness;
For that there is no need to take my pulse,
Because the pain is anchored deep in my spirit;
I'm ill because I'm filled with the love of God.
He alone can cure me.

You cannot treat me until you get rid of the evil that is troubling you within;
When you are cured, only then can you call yourself a doctor.

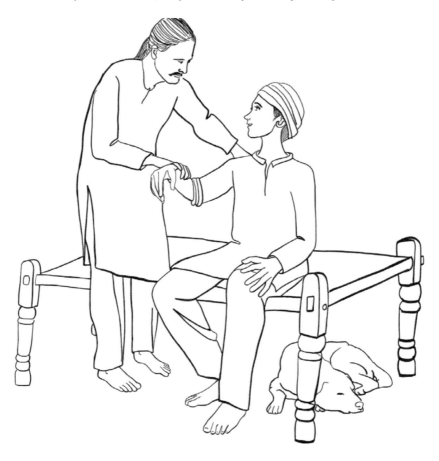

The doctor smiled knowingly because he was also used to treating the mentally ill.

"So, you think that I should get treatment?"

"Certainly," replied Nanak. "Your soul is sick. Your ego is the cause. It separates us not only from our neighbours but also from the source of life, God himself."

Suddenly Hari Das felt bathed in a sense of peace he had never experienced before. He was stupefied by the truth the young sick person had uttered.

"You are talking about spiritual matters; I deal with problems of the body," the doctor responded.

Nanak looked at him graciously and replied, "The body is good for nothing if the spirit within it is unhealthy."

"That's true," the doctor admitted. "But how is it that this truth escapes human beings? Is there no hope? What is the treatment?" Hari Das asked.

"The disease is called the evil. It can be cured when God showers his grace on human beings. This is the only cure."

Forgetting his doctor's role, Hari Das tried to absorb in his mind the divine perfume that Nanak exhaled. He bowed before Nanak and left without prescribing any medicine, telling Kalu, "Don't worry, your son himself is a supreme healer."

Endnote: Nanak wrote the poem many years later, so the story appears to have been invented.

11. STOREKEEPER

Do you remember Nanak's older sister Nanki? She and her husband Jai Ram lived in Sultanpur, a big city. As they could not have any children, Nanki was much attached to her brother. She told her husband about Nanak's strange illness. They decided to visit him and their parents. Nanki worried much about her father's anxiety. After discussing it with the family, she suggested to her brother, "I know you are not interested in business. Why don't you work for the government? My husband works there and can find a suitable position for you. Come stay with us in Sultanpur." Nanak liked the idea and gladly agreed.

Kalu was greatly relieved. He trusted his daughter. Jai Ram had no problem finding him employment as a storekeeper in a food store of the governor, Nabob Daulat Khan. In those times, farmers paid taxes directly to the government. As they did not have money, they gave as tax a part of their harvest of wheat, cotton, sugar or spices. These were stored in a large storehouse.

The village chief, Rai Bular, organized a great farewell feast for Nanak. The entire village came to wish him good luck. But Nanak's wife, Sulakhani, was very sad. She wept as she said to Nanak, "You have always ignored me. What will become of me? Who will take care of me?"

Nanak replied, "Don't be naïve. Wherever I am, your situation will not change."

"I do not want to stay here without you! Please take me with you."

Nanak consoled her, "All right, I go now. If I earn enough, God willing, I'll send for you and you can join me. Please accept this arrangement."

His wife remained silent. After hugging everyone he left for Sultanpur.

Jai Ram took him to the Nabob, who was greatly impressed by Nanak. "I like him very much. He seems to be an honest man. He will be responsible for our Modikhana, our storehouse."

Then he spoke to Nanak, "You'll distribute rations justly among my family, soldiers, police, and the employees. The remaining stock you'll sell to people. Keep an account of all sales."

Nanak worked diligently and enjoyed it. That made his sister very happy. He liked helping the poor. If a beggar went there, he would not go away empty-handed. Soon people started to talk about Nanak's kindness. In spite of that, many evil tongues reported to the Nabob quite the opposite. "Your storekeeper is dishonest and negligent. Soon your store will be empty."

The Nabob ordered his officers to check the accounts. They found that Nanak had kept them meticulously, with no errors. More and more people began to praise Nanak for being an honest storekeeper.

He also helped the governor to reduce corruption among other officers, who had a habit of keeping ten percent of what they distributed or sold. By then his wife had joined him. They lived in a rented house. Nanki was very happy that her brother was doing so well. One day she proposed to him that they start a family. Actually, she herself longed to bring up one of his children because she could not have her own. Nanak was never against starting a family. Do you remember that he was sixteen years old when he married Sulakhani in 1484? When Nanak was twenty-seven, a son was born who was named Sri Chand. A little later, Nanak was blessed with another son, Lakhmi Das. Apparently, Nanak wanted to show that having a family is no obstacle to leading a spiritual life.

Every day after finishing his work, Nanak would bathe in the River Bein and then join other villagers to sing hymns. They felt that they needed a good musician.

Nanak sent a message to his friend Mardana, who came without delay. Being from a clan of musicians, Mardana was a good musician. Soon Nanak's house became a refuge for beggars, fakirs and the helpless, who turned up to appease their hunger and talk with Nanak. One day Nanak's mother-in-law spoke to his sister Nanki, "Nanak must first take care of the needs of his own family before giving charity."

"He manages his affairs well. At the end of the month he has enough left for the family," Nanki replied.

12. DROWNED IN THE RIVER

It may appear that Nanak lived a peaceful life. But the stars announced a great upheaval. One early morning, Nanak and a friend went to bathe in the River Bein, about two kilometres from his house. The soothing beauty of the place attracted many bathers. That day he left his clothes with his friend and plunged into the river. Carried off by the current, Nanak disappeared. A considerable time passed, but he did not reappear. Some onlookers thought he had drowned. Some evil wishers said, "He must have stolen something from the storehouse and now out of guilt he has deliberately jumped into the river."

In the river Nanak had encountered some angels, who led him to God. One of the angels announced respectfully, "Nanak presents himself to You."

Meanwhile, on the bank, Nanak's friend became worried. Picking up his clothes, he ran to tell the Nabob. "Sir, Nanak has not come out of the river. I think he has drowned."

Daulat Khan mounted his horse and galloped to the river. He called the fishermen; they quickly spread their fishing nets to find Nanak. Sadly, the nets came up empty. Many minutes passed; any hope of finding him diminished and then died completely, giving way to grim reality.

"He was an honest officer," Nabob lamented.

This gentle and kind-hearted person, father of a family, had drowned and his body could not be found. It was a terrible loss for his many friends.

Now as we know, Nanak was not dead at all, but standing in front of God. He presented himself, "I am your servant, and I'm ready to follow your will."

God handed him a bowl. "Drink this nectar in my Name."

The effect of the delicious nectar spread throughout Nanak's senses. In kindness, God watched him drink and said, "Go and contemplate Name and teach others to do the same. It is important that you learn to detach yourself from material pleasures while living in the world. Live in the state of the Name, charity, service and contemplation. This will be your task."

When Nanak bowed and got up, God asked him, "What do you think of the glory of the Name?"

Inspired, Nanak started to sing a beautiful melody:

Were my life to extend millions of millions of years,
And if the air could satisfy my thirst and hunger;
If hiding in a cave I saw neither moon nor sun;
If there were no place to sleep even in my dreams;
Even then I would not be able to know Your worth;
Nor could I say how great is Your Name.

Greatly pleased, God responded, "You have understood well my instruction. Now for you to act."

God encouraged him, "Your look of grace will be my look of grace; your benevolent action will be mine. And you are a supreme guru."

Nanak bowed at God's feet and received his blessing.

At the end of three days, the angels took Nanak back to the riverbank. When Nanak suddenly emerged from the water, the people were stupefied and could not believe their eyes. Nanak looked like a changed person.

"What happened to you? Where were you?" people asked.

Nanak remained silent. He was wearing only a loincloth.

"Surely he was injured in the river," someone said.

13. NO HINDU, NO MUSLIM

Do you think Nanak really spent three days at the bottom of the river and met God? Some say that in fact Nanak swam across the river to the other bank and remained in some calm spot in the forest contemplating. Nevertheless, when he appeared from the river like a phantom it was a moment of great joy for all. Everyone marvelled at the light emanating from his face. All noticed the divine aura surrounding his figure. His transformation surprised everyone. He became a living master, cast in divine light and ready to respond to the pressing needs of humanity.

On the first day, Nanak spoke to no one. A crowd gathered around him, and he uttered his first words: "There is no Hindu and no Muslim." Someone reported to Daulat Khan what Nanak was saying.

"Don't worry about Nanak; he has become a hermit," said the Khan.

Sitting near him was the Qazi, the judge of Sultanpur. He reacted differently, "O great Khan, it is nevertheless quite strange for him to say that there is no Hindu nor Muslim."

The Khan then ordered his officer to bring Nanak to him. "Nanak, in the name of Allah, the Khan wants to see you."

"I've nothing to tell him," Nanak replied.

On hearing his words, people said, "He's gone berserk. He is mad."

Nanak asked Mardana to beat a rhythm and he sang a song:

Some call me a phantom;
Others say I am a demon;
Some claim I'm a poor clumsy person;
I, Nanak, have fallen madly in love with the divine Name;
I recognize nothing other than God.

When he finished singing, Nanak said, "Now my Master wants me to see the Khan."

Seeing Nanak in an ascetic's robe and wearing wooden beads around his neck, the Khan said, "For God's sake, remove that necklace and your hermit's belt."

Nanak removed them both. The Khan continued, "I'm very sad that my excellent officer has become an ascetic."

Then he made Nanak sit next to him. "Now, Qazi, ask him your questions."

Laughing loudly the Qazi turned to Nanak, "You claim that there is no Hindu and no Muslim. Where have you learned that? You lie. There are thousands of Muslims. I do not even talk about Hindus."

Nanak replied, "Before God, all human beings are equal, whether Hindu or Muslim. There is no difference between the followers of these two faiths. To God they are equal. Each one appears before him only with the deeds he has done during his stay on this earth."

"Then tell me, how many are true Hindus and true Muslims?"

Nanak replied, "To that I say that there is no distinction between the practices of the two faiths."

Nanak had understood the concept of human brotherhood and the fatherhood of God. His message was well above ceremonies and rituals that priests had set up. He addressed everyone without taking into account religion, race or colour.

14. NANAK GOES TO THE MOSQUE AND LEAVES HIS FAMILY

The Qazi was so stunned that he did not know what to say. But he was irritated by Nanak's behaviour and found his talk ridiculous. Overcome by anger, he reacted with a voice of authority: "Perhaps Hindus are bad messengers of their faith, but we Muslims say our prayer five times a day, and we are the true devotees of the prophet Mohammad."

Nanak thought calmly and replied lovingly:

Five prayers with different names
Five times a day,
But if the truth were your first prayer,
Honestly earning your daily bread, the second,
Sharing your meal in the Name of God, the third;
Purifying your mind, the fourth;
Adoring God, the fifth…
If you practice these five virtues,
All mingled with good actions,
Only then can you call yourself a true Muslim.

That made Qazi angrier. He heard the Mullah's call from the mosque for namaz, the afternoon prayer. When the judge became very nervous, the Khan, a virtuous person full of curiosity, intervened and questioned Nanak,

"If, in your eyes, all religions are the same, would you join us in our prayer?"

"I would love it," Nanak replied.

His brother-in-law, Jai Ram, who had listened to the conversation, told his wife, Nanki, "I'm worried that Nanak might convert to Islam."

"No, I know my brother. That will never happen," she assured him.

The mosque was full of worshipers praising Allah and thus fulfilling the requirement of their religion. However, one person remained still and did not participate in the ritual. Nanak took a quick look at the Qazi and smiled. When the namaz ended, the Qazi complained to the Khan, "Did you see how this Hindu is making fun of us? And you say Nanak is a good person." Then he turned to Nanak and said, "You are nothing but an imposter. You promised that you would pray with us, but you make fun of us!"

"What have you to say, Nanak?" the Khan asked.

"Great Khan, after listening to you I promised to offer my prayer with you. But how could I do that when the Qazi was not even there?"

"What are you talking? I was praying with you," the Qazi replied angrily.

"I smiled at you because your mind was quite far away from your words while you were praying."

"Explain yourself," the Khan demanded.

"Well, while Qazi's body seemed to be praying," Nanak clarified, "his thoughts were completely absorbed in fear that his new-born foal might fall into the pit in his back yard. How could I join him in prayer if the Qazi was not praying?"

Flustered, the judge lowered his head. What Nanak said was correct.

"And you," he turned to the Khan, "You were also absent, thinking about your dealers who are now buying horses in Kabul!"

"Yes, Qazi, Nanak is right. I've nothing to say."

The Khan and his Qazi and the other worshippers bowed to Nanak, who began to recite:

Those who contemplate with total devotion receive God's grace.

People started to spread the story, "God speaks through Nanak."

The Khan offered Nanak all his possessions. But Nanak declined and declared, "As for me, I abandon everything." He left and joined some sadhus. Then he withdrew to an isolated place. This aroused much curiosity. All kinds of people came from far away to see him. Some made remarks. They thought that a wicked spirit had possessed Nanak; others said that he had gone crazy.

Jai Ram was deeply troubled. He called a Maulavi, a Muslim wise man, who assured him that by using his power to exorcise he would cure Nanak. The Maulavi started chanting and then ordered the bad spirit to show itself. Nanak smiled at this comedy and said, "This poor man claims that whoever does not recognize God is possessed by evil."

"You talk like a sage but act like an idiot," the Maulavi said.

"You consider me to be an imbecile because I consider worthless everything that you and others think to be important?" Nanak said.

After reflecting a little Maulavi said, "You have a holy spirit. But what moves you to leave your family?"

"I want to serve the world."

Nanki tried to persuade her brother to stay with his wife and children. "My dear sister, all human beings are my family, and I their servant. I also serve God. I place my family in God's hands. I must go wherever he wants me to go. But every time you think of me, I will be at your side."

Then he approached his tearful wife, who fell at his feet shaking with sobs. Nanak placed his hand on her head. Her despair turned at once to serenity and calm. She saw a vision that caused her to say, "O my lord and master, go. The world is on fire. Go and extinguish this fire that is consuming it."

On that day, Nanak left his family and departed with his faithful companion Mardana. Jai Ram and Nanki—she did not have any children—took the elder son, Sri Chand. His wife Sulakhani went to live with her parents along with the younger son, Lakhmi Das.

15. HOW MARDANA FOUND HIS REBAB

When they had scarcely started walking, Nanak told Mardana, "Go north. On the way you will meet a friend who will hand you a musical instrument called a rebab." Mardana was stunned. He did not know anyone in that direction, nor did he know how to play a rebab. But sensing the sincerity in Nanak's eyes, he left and headed north.

After walking a short distance, he reached a village called Bharoana. He scrutinized the faces of the people he saw, but no one paid any attention to him. Then a man named Phiranda stopped in front of him and asked, "What are you looking for?"

"A rebab," said Mardana.

"It looks as though Nanak has sent you here," said the stranger. "Tell him that his servant has done what he wanted. Here is the instrument that I have safeguarded for you for many years. Blessed be those who have had the opportunity of enjoying the guru's company."

Mardana returned to Nanak, who asked him to play the rebab. But Mardana had never played the rebab. The only instrument he knew how to play was the flute. "But how do I play this?" Mardana moaned.

Nanak started to sing. Mardana placed the bow on a string. The rebab had only three strings. Mardana was amazed at his own dexterity. It seemed as if he'd possessed an inspired virtuosity all the time. Nanak continued to sing. This became Nanak's way of sharing his teaching throughout their long journeys.

Endnote: Mardana was actually born into a musician caste and learned to play various instruments and sing well from a very young age.

16. MARDANA CARRIES A BUNDLE ON HIS HEAD

The three of them—Nanak, Mardana and Bala—began their first fantastic journey. Do you remember that Bala had gone with Nanak to the market to make a good bargain? At the start of their trek they avoided the villages and spent nights in the forests or on riverbanks. One day Nanak asked Mardana, "Are you hungry?"

"Why do you ask me, when you know everything?"

Nanak continued, "Follow this track until you arrive at the house of a merchant named Uppal. Stand there without making any noise. You will notice that whoever sees you, Hindu or Muslim, will bow down to you. You will receive dozens of offerings of all kinds, as well as rupees and silk scarves. Nobody will ask you where you have come from."

That's exactly what happened. People said, "We are blessed to have met you." Mardana felt embarrassed and uneasy. He did not know what to do with all these offerings. Finally, he made a big bundle of the scarves, placed it on his head and returned to the forest where Nanak was waiting. Seeing him, Nanak doubled over with laughter.

"What have you brought?"

"Thanks to you, the whole village seemed excited and offered a mountain of things and even worshipped me. They gave me much to eat. I have brought some clothes only. I thought we might need them. ."

"Thank you, you have thought well. But they will not be of any use to us."

"What do you want me to do now?"

"Throw them all away!"

"Come, play the rebab. We'll sing together."
Then they continued on their journey.

17. LALO, THE POOR CARPENTER

At the end of the first stage of their quest, Nanak and his companions stopped in Saidpur, where they found a place to stay in the simple house of Lalo, a poor carpenter of a lower caste. Even though Lalo could not offer much comfort, he was very happy and honoured by the visit of such a saintly person. After listening to the divine message, the carpenter felt spiritually uplifted. In the evening Lalo could offer only small beds.

As always, Mardana felt hungry. With much love, Lalo's wife prepared chapattis and lentils and served her guests. Seeing the rough and thick chapattis, Mardana hesitated to eat them, fearing that he might break his teeth. But as he was dying of hunger and saw that Nanak was relishing them, he dared to take a bite. He closed his eyes and murmured ecstatically, "Delicious! It's sweeter than milk and honey."

After a few days Mardana returned to Talvandi, about forty kilometres away, to marry off his daughter. While Mardana was gone, Nanak planned and prepared for his long journey. During the day he walked in the forest, ate little and meditated as he sat on stones. Many people were attracted by Nanak's radiant personality, grace and simplicity. In the evening these people gathered in front of Lalo's house to listen to Nanak and discuss all kinds of social and work issues.

The people of upper caste, Brahmins and Kshatriyas, did not like Nanak. One of the Kshatriyas shouted at him, "How dare you have a Muslim as your companion, live with a low caste person and share his food? Nanak, you are on the wrong path. This is not expected of a Hindu."

Endnote: Lalo lived in Saidpur (Eminabad). He was a carpenter of Ghataura caste and was Nanak's first disciple. Nanak stayed with him for many days. He had only one child, a daughter, whose descendants still live in Tatla village.

18. MILK AND BLOOD

When Mardana came back, both he and Nanak sang songs that Nanak had composed: They spelled out four goals: never forget God, earn your bread honestly, live truthfully and help the poor.

For many Hindus and Muslims, Nanak became a source of hope and inspiration. It is said that Lalo was his first disciple (Sikh). During Nanak's stay with Lalo, a rich noble of the region, Malik Bhago, was preparing a great feast of sacrifice. He invited all holy men of all castes living in the region to eat the brahmbhoj, the sacred meal. This noble was a corrupt man and of bad nature. He inflicted much hardship on poor citizens and used all sorts of dishonest excuses to take away their money. In order to show that he was an honourable man he organized feasts like the one to which Nanak and his friends were also invited.

Malik Bhago's servant announced, "Nanak, you and your companions are invited to the noble's feast."

Nanak declined the invitation.

"This will greatly sadden Malik Bhago. His feast will be incomplete if a saintly man like you refuses to participate."

The sadhus of high caste who accompanied the servant cursed Nanak. "He's nothing but a fakir who eats with people of lower caste."

When the servant informed Malik Bhago of Nanak's response, he quickly sent his personal assistant to convince Nanak. After much insisting, Nanak agreed to go to the festival accompanied by Lalo.

Nanak said to Lalo, "I see that you still have one chapatti left over from this morning. Bring it with you."

Malik Bhago was delighted to see Nanak and his companions coming, followed by many workers. He received them with a big dish filled with succulent delicacies. "O holy man, why do you refuse to eat such delicious food? You're quite strange. You live with this poor carpenter and you eat with low caste people!"

"I do not belong to any caste, and I love the food that Lalo serves me. I do not like your meal," Nanak answered.

"Why not?" Bhago asked, quite upset.

Nanak smiled and looking at the food dish said, "I can't share your meal because it's poisoned."

These words, spoken in front of the whole gathering, did not please the noble at all. "How can you say that? Prove it to me," retorted Bhago angrily.

Nanak took Lalo's chapatti in his right hand and another chapatti from Bhago's kitchen in his left hand. When he squeezed them in his hands at the same time, milk dripped from his right hand and blood from the left hand.

"You see, your chapatti has been made from the blood you have sucked from the poor, whereas Lalo's chapatti was cooked with milk earned honestly by hard work. Lalo shares what he earns with others. His food is pure. It's delicious, like milk and honey. You have forced people to work for you, and you take away all that they produce. They are always hungry. What you eat is soaked with their blood. Tell me, how can I eat your meal?"

Hearing this, the noble was stunned and felt terribly guilty.

"I deeply repent my past actions and seek your forgiveness and grace," he begged.

Nanak instructed him, "Distribute all the wealth you acquired with your evil schemes. From now on, try to live honestly, with love and service."

Then he added, "Just as a Muslim is forbidden to eat pork or a Hindu to eat beef, it is forbidden to take what belongs to others!"

The story of this incident spread to the four corners of the country. From that day, the noble Malik Bhago changed into an honest man completely devoted to doing good work.

19. SAJJAN, THE FRIEND-SWINDLER

Nanak continued his journey with his friends Bala and Mardana from village to village, always enlightening the hearts of people. One day Mardana asked Nanak, "Master, many pilgrims go to Pakpatan for Ziarat, pilgrimage, to the tomb of Sheikh Farid Shakarganj. I too would like to go there."

"Why not! That way we can meet his successor, Sheikh Ibrahim," said Nanak. "After that we'll continue to Multan and even to Uch, the third Muslim sacred place."

In those days, to go from Saidpur to Pakpatan one took the road to Lahore and then to Multan. After walking for a number of days they reached the town of Tulamba on the bank of the Ravi. But they could not find an inn to spend the night. A little farther they came to an inn run by a man named Sajjan. He welcomed all travellers, offering them a meal and sweet talk. The word sajjan means a good friend. Charmed by the beauty of the place, Nanak decided to spend the night there. They saw Sajjan, elegantly dressed in white, continuously counting the beads of a rosary. He welcomed Hindus with hands respectfully joined and offered salaam to Muslims with his hand touching his heart. No one could imagine that Sajjan was a veritable incarnation of the devil. He was a thief and killer. After serving a delicious dinner to his guests he would take them to their rooms. Tired, they would quickly go to sleep. During their sleep he would kill them, then throw their bodies into a deep well and take their belongings. Nanak knew all this; he wanted to teach Sajjan a lesson.

"What is your name?" Nanak asked him.

"Hindus call me Sajjan Mal and Muslims call me Sajjan Shah. But I'm neither Hindu nor Muslim. I'm simply Sajjan, a friend and a servant of people."

"Truly? Do you really behave like a friend?"

"I serve my guests with devotion. I feed them and lodge them free of charge. Have you noticed that I've built a pretty little temple on the right side of the entrance for Hindus and a mosque on the left for Muslims, with separate pots filled with water so that visitors can refresh themselves at leisure?" But even while speaking these words, Sajjan was thinking how easy it would be to get rid of these defenceless guests. Sajjan said to his servants, "His talk is so refined. His eyes seem to say that he knows the world. He must have a lot money. Surely, he is hiding, disguised as a fakir."

Sajjan served food to his three guests, showing much humility. It was already quite late and Sajjan became impatient.

"My good friends," he said, "you must be tired after such a long journey. A little sleep will do you good. Your well-rested legs will feel light on the journey that awaits you in the morning."

Nanak replied, "The time to rest has not yet come. If you need to go to sleep, please go ahead. We'll sleep according to God's wish. Sajjan, before going to bed we are going to pray."

Then Nanak asked Mardana to play the rebab. In the silence of the night the sound of the rebab and Nanak's melody touched Sajjan's heart. The song described the qualities of a good friend.

The stork robed in white feathers
Lives in holy pilgrimage places;
But he catches innocent creatures and swallows them;
He cannot be called a friend.

Each verse fulfilled its aim, and one by one Sajjan's deeds were revealed. His conscience was deeply shaken as he thought about his diabolical crimes. He fell at Nanak's feet, weeping bitterly, and implored him, "How can I be forgiven?"

Raising the sinner's head, Nanak told him, "O, Sheikh Sajjan, you have two ways to obtain pardon."

"Tell me. I'll obey you," said Sajjan in desperation.

Nanak asked him, "Tell the truth; how many have you killed?"

Sajjan answered honestly, "I've sinned a lot. What should I do?"

"You must first recognize your mistakes deep in your heart and regret them sincerely. Then find the families of your victims. Return to them what belongs to them and seek their forgiveness." Nanak then showed him life's true path.

From then on Sajjan transformed his inn into a dharamsala, a resting place for travellers and the poor. It was the first place of this kind in the region.

The three travellers left the bank of the River Ravi, crossed the River Sutlej in a boat and reached Pakpatan. It was called Ajodhan in those days. This town was founded by Sheikh Farid, a Sufi born in Persia in 1173. It was here that he met a Hindu yogi named Bir Nath, who converted to Islam and changed his name to Pir Kamal. Pir is a title given to a spiritual master belonging to the Muslim Sufi sect. Nanak and his companions camped a little outside the town. On that day Pir Kamal was collecting firewood in the forest. He heard someone singing. He approached a small clearing and saw Mardana playing the rebab as Nanak sang along with him:

You are unique, there is no one else like you.

Pir Kamal put down his bundle and asked the two singers to repeat these words, and he memorized them. He thanked them with a salaam, lifted his firewood and left hurriedly.

"O, Pir, I've just met Allah's beloved," Kamal announced, quite breathless. Then he described everything to his master Pir Sheikh Ibrahim. "A Hindu fakir singing his own songs invoking Islamic principles: 'there is but one God."

"That is strange—a Hindu singing of a unique God!" Ibrahim responded. "Can you take me to these people?"

"Certainly."

The two men went to see Nanak in the forest. "Salaam alaykum," Ibrahim greeted Nanak.

"Alaykum salaam to you," Nanak replied.

Ibrahim took them to his monastery and invited them to stay there. They discussed and shared their spiritual ideas. When they finished,

Nanak agreed, "A fickle mind is the root of all problems. It must be kept in check."

The sheikh laughed, "I need a knife to kill the fickle mind."

Nanak replied:

The Name is the knife and the steel that it's made of;
Sharpened on the grindstone of Word, it is placed in the furnace of truth;
If you are killed by it, you will see your blood flushing out greed;
By becoming hallal you will be united with the Eternal.

Then Nanak took his leave in order to continue his trek. He said, "My dear Ibrahim, I had such pleasure talking with you. God willing, I'd love to see you again."

Endnote. Hallal refers to what is permissible or lawful in traditional Islamic law.

20. MULTAN, THE CITY OF MUSLIM PROPHETS

Not far from Pakpatan there are two other sacred cities of Sufis, Multan and Uch. After a few days' march, the three comrades saw the great city of Multan on the horizon. Many Sufis visit this place. Nanak and his companions sat down near the tomb of Pir Baha-ud-Din, a deeply respected, saintly man.

When the current Pir came to know that there was a travelling fakir nearby, he sent one of his disciples to Nanak with a bowl filled to the brim with milk. Without a word, the messenger offered the bowl to Nanak. Nanak calmly picked a jasmine flower and, floating it delicately on the milk, said, "Take this bowl of milk back to your master."

Curious as always, Mardana asked, "What does this signify?"

"The Pir wants to tell us that the city is already full of saintly people, like the milk in the bowl, and that there is no place there for us. I simply want to tell him that I will be like the jasmine flower floating on the milk."

Pir found Nanak's response amusing and came with others to meet him. After the usual salutations all of them sat down in the shade of nearby trees.

"Where do you come from? What is your religion?" the Pir asked.

"I come from the place we all come from, the source of all existence. I belong to his religion."

"Do you believe that God is the source of everything?" the Pir inquired with a provocative look.

Nanak looked into his eyes and explained that God is present in everything, and he is nearer to us than one thinks.

"I do not doubt your sincerity and wisdom," the Pir replied, "I see an aura of light around your head."

Their discussion continued in the lodge for a number of days. The Pir was pleased to learn much from Nanak. To the Pir's great regret, Nanak decided to continue his trek. The Pir proposed that Nanak stay a little longer; but Nanak replied, "It would be simple to install oneself on a permanent basis and thus avoid the trouble and worries of moving daily. But to my way of thinking, it's better to travel and benefit during life on earth in order to encounter God."

21. MARDANA TIRED

After travelling for a few months, Nanak and his companions returned to Punjab to see their families. Nanak was thirty years old. He was already well known in the region. Many people came to listen to his teachings. Soon he was ready to undertake a long, fantastic journey that would last twelve years. Nanak departed from Sultanpur in 1499, accompanied by his two friends, Bala, a Hindu, and Mardana, a Muslim. Nanak dressed in a saffron coloured Hindu toga and placed a white one in his bag. He wore flat leather sandals and put in his bag a pair of wooden clogs like those of fakirs and yogis. He put a scarf round his neck and covered his head with a cap commonly worn by Hindu hermits. In his hand he held a rosary of bones, and he painted his forehead with saffron like a proper yogi.

Do you believe that Nanak actually dressed like this? Surely, he did not. He wasn't a wizard but an extremely humble person. His brain was full of ideas for subtly correcting people who dressed like that. The three friends wore simple rustic clothes and robust shoes in preparation for any hazard that might befall them during the journey.

The first person they met was a Muslim saint, Sheikh Sayyad, who sat in a palanquin carried by four weak and tired-looking porters wearing only loincloths. They placed the palanquin gently under a tree where two of them quickly began massaging the sheikh's legs and arms while others started to fan him.

Already tired, Mardana was deeply discouraged at this sight and asked Nanak, "Is there really only one God?"

"Of course, Mardana."

"But where does this sheikh come from who travels in such comfort, without working and with so many looking after him?"

"You see, in this world, power is superior to spirituality, and hell is the ruler." Mardana understood what Nanak meant and continued walking without complaint.

22. QUENCHING THE THIRST OF ANCESTORS LIVING ON THE SUN

Our three travellers crossed the River Sutlej and took the road towards Delhi. They visited the Hindu holy place called Pehowa, where flowed the mythical River Sarasvati in very ancient times. On the day of solar eclipse, they reached Kurukshetra. This was the theatre of the famous battle of Mahabharata. A great many yogis and hermits had assembled to celebrate the eclipse festival.

Nanak had just camped on a high ground when a prince returning from hunting passed by and wanted to meet him. Ignoring the fact that it was the sacred eclipse day, he offered Nanak a deer he had killed. Mardana quickly lit a fire. Nanak placed an earthenware cooking pot on it to cook the deer meat. When the yogis saw the smoke and smelled the odour of meat, they rushed towards them, full of anger.

"How dare you cook meat on this sacred day," exclaimed Nanu Mal, one of the pundits. He was very clever in the art of discussion and the furious crowd supported him.

Nanak said in a calm voice, "One should not quarrel on this sacred day." Then he sang:

First a human being is conceived in flesh (semen);
Then it lives in flesh (uterus);
When it takes form, its mouth takes in flesh;
Its bones are enveloped with flesh and skin, forming the body;
When flesh of the uterus pushes it out, its mouth of flesh sucks the breast of flesh;
Its mouth is flesh, its tongue is flesh, it breathes through flesh;
It grows and marries and brings home flesh;
Flesh is produced from flesh, all parents are made of flesh.

Only fools discuss flesh and meat, but they know nothing of spiritual learning and contemplation;
They do not know the difference between meat and vegetables, or where sin resides.

These words calmed Nanu Mal and his friends, who then left.

Our travellers continued their journey, crossed the River Yamuna and one day reached Hardwar on the bank of the River Ganges, the most sacred for Hindus. In those days, this place was not littered by houses.

The following day was the spring festival. At sunrise our travellers went to the sacred river to see what was happening. They saw thousands of Hindus, accompanied by their priests, bathing and performing religious rituals. Standing in the river, they filled their cupped hands with water and threw it towards the rising sun. Nanak smiled and approached a priest. Very innocently he asked the priest, "My dear friends, what are you doing?"

"Don't tell me that you do not know! We are offering water to our dead ancestors."

"But why?"

"They are very thirsty; we must quench their thirst."

"Where do they live?"

"You poor naïve man. They live on the sun."

Nanak thought about this a little and then waded into the river. He, too, took water in his cupped hands, closed his eyes, and threw it in the same manner, but much faster and in the opposite direction. The horrified pilgrims and priests gathered around him and asked, "What are you doing? Have you gone mad?"

"I'm watering my fields, which are in Punjab near Lahore. I've received news that it has not rained since my departure," Nanak replied in a convincing tone. "I was sad to learn that I was going to lose my crops. That is why I'm using your method. But instead of throwing with only one hand, I'm using both hands so that my field will be watered quickly and saved. Thank you—now please let me continue my work!"

Amused by this reply, the crowd laughed loudly. One shouted, "O ignorant man, are you out of your mind? How can you make your water reach your fields so far away from here? Don't you see, water falls from your hands in the river at your feet?"

"You are correct. You are truly wise. At what distance do your ancestors live?" Nanak asked.

"Very far, in the world beyond, millions of kilometres away," one of them answered.

"If this water in my hands cannot reach my fields, which are on this earth a few kilometres away, how do you expect the water that you offer to your ancestors to reach them? They are not even alive and therefore are not physically troubled by hunger or thirst," said Nanak.

Then he turned to the priests, "You have abandoned the correct divine way. You claim that you can ensure a place in paradise for those who have disappeared from this world simply by throwing water in the direction of the sun and performing useless ceremonies."

The pilgrims standing around liked what Nanak said, but the priests did not. One of the priests shouted, "What right do you have to talk like this? Your talk will take you directly to hell. We are Brahmins, and we worship our gods and goddesses as we have been taught. We follow strictly what our sacred books command us to do."

Nanak smiled a little and replied:

Those who perform ceremonies without love of God and humanity in their hearts;
And who accept money in return, are condemned.

While the pilgrims listened to Nanak attentively, the disillusioned priests withdrew, one after the other.

Our three friends followed the road that took them to Delhi. Northern India up to Delhi had been conquered by the Turks. When Nanak arrived there, Sultan Ibrahim Beg was on the throne. The three companions stayed in the quarter of the mahouts, the caretakers of elephants. The simple and honest mahouts welcomed the visitors lovingly. But when our friends were resting, the sound of people crying in the street woke them up. Nanak went outside and asked the people, "Why are you crying like this?"

"It's because of the elephant that has just fallen dead," a mahout replied.

"Who does it belong to?"

"It belongs to the sultan, and it's his favourite."

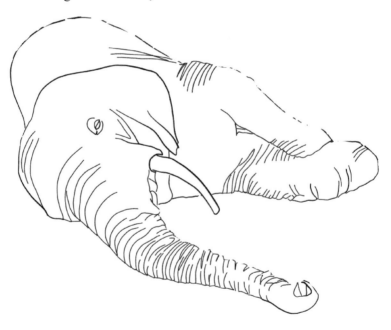

"That is no reason to cry," Nanak said.

"But the sultan will be angry with us, and then I'll lose my job."

"Then find another job," Nanak advised.

"I adore working as a mahout, and my salary allows me to feed my family well. Besides, I don't know any other work."

"If this elephant is alive again, will you stop crying?"

"But how can it be? It's dead!"

"You'll soon understand," said Nanak. "Go and caress its head while you repeat 'God is wonderful'."

What a surprise! The elephant opened its eyes and stood up. Everyone was wonderstruck. The news quickly reached the ear of the sultan. He ordered that the elephant be brought to him. Seated on the elephant, the sultan came to see Nanak.

"Oh, dervish, is it you who revived my elephant?"

"Life and death are in God's hand, and the prayer of a fakir depends on Allah's grace."

"Now show me how you will put it to death."

Nanak replied with a couplet:

It is He who causes life and death;
I have nothing other than the Unique.

At that very moment the elephant fell to the ground and lay dead and stiff.

"Revive it now," the sultan commanded.

Nanak explained to him: "O great Sultan, iron becomes red in the fire. This heat cannot be held in the hand. How can the heat remain red? In the same way, fakirs are aglow with God's heat. They cannot raise what God has brought down."

The sultan understood Nanak's message that performing miracles is against God's will. We leave nature to take its course. The sultan, happy and satisfied, wanted to offer something to Nanak, but he refused: "I am thirsty for Allah only, and I have a craving to see him." Our three friends left the sultan and resumed their journey.

Endnote: Being a very observant person, Nanak noticed that the elephant had collapsed because it was very tired. It got up when the mahout caressed it. Carrying the sultan after that exhausted the elephant and so it died.

23. POISONOUS CHERRIES

Hardwar was the starting point of many pilgrimage routes towards the Himalayas, the highest mountain range on earth. Our three friends, Nanak, Bala and Mardana, followed a sinuous route that passed through dense forests full of tigers, lions, elephants, rhinoceroses, and all kinds of venomous snakes. They met peace-loving people as well as savages and even cannibals. They also saw harmless animals, like deer, hares, and all kinds of colourful birds singing in the trees. The beauty of nature and the tranquillity induced many people to meditate and do penance in order to find peace, reach God, or understand life. These people were known as yogis or rishis—hermits and monks. They lived in twelve distinct groups in separate monasteries or hermitages. The trio followed the track through thick, humid forest towards Badrinath and Kedarnath, two Hindu sacred places. They crossed western Nepal and descended to the River Sharda or Kali (Black). They halted under a tree where the track divided.

As always, someone had a problem—surely it was Mardana.

"Master, you're a godly person, and hunger and thirst do not affect you. But I, I'm just a simple mortal who needs to eat. I feel very weak. I'm hungry. It's quite a few days that we haven't eaten. I don't have the strength to take even one more step."

"Follow the track on the left," advised Nanak. "Not far from here you'll come to a cottage of yogis. Ask them for something to eat."

Mardana trudged on, and soon he saw smoke rising from a cottage. He asked a yogi whether he might have something to eat.

"Who are you? A beggar? Who has sent you here?" the yogi asked.

"My master, Nanak."

"If you have a master, then tell him to give you food. Go away."

Discouraged, Mardana took the return track and reported to Nanak what had happened.

Near them was a soap-berry tree loaded with ripe fruit like cherries. "Climb this tree and eat its fruit. Be careful, don't bring any with you," said Nanak.

Mardana looked at the tree. He knew that its cherries were very bitter, like the nuts often used for washing clothes. He hesitated, knowing that the cherries were inedible. But he also knew that Nanak never lied. Reluctantly, he climbed the tree. He was astonished to find that the cherries were delicious. They melted in his mouth like a fudge. He ate a lot. His hunger satisfied, he forgot Nanak's instruction and put some cherries in his pocket. Next morning, he was hungry again. He ate the

cherries from his pocket. Almost immediately he started to vomit and lost his voice.

Nanak laughed at him and said, "That's what happens when one is greedy. You did not even think of sharing them with Bala. A good lesson for you."

Poor Mardana sought forgiveness. He reached out his hands, knelt in front of Nanak with tears in his eyes, and asked to be pardoned. Nanak touched Mardana's head, and at once he found his voice.

The three resumed their journey on a tortuous fifty-kilometre track that brought them to Gorakhmatta, the country of the Dharu tribe. Nanak rested in the shade of a huge poplar tree.

Nanak asked Mardana to get fire from the yogis, but they refused. Mardana succeeded in finding fire elsewhere and lit it under the same tree. Again, according to the legend, a strong wind started up and brought much rain with it during the night. The fires of all the yogis were extinguished, but Mardana's was not. The jealous and angry yogis tried but failed to burn the poplar tree. But in the end, they recognized their error and came to seek forgiveness from Nanak.

According to a local legend, from that day on every leaf of this tree carries a print of Nanak's hand. The leaves are dark green and thicker than those of a normal poplar.

"Who is your master? Who has initiated you?" they asked Nanak. Nanak replied with a song:

My beloved Master is infused in water, in the earth and in the upper and lower universes;
He instils all.

The yogis insisted: "You must become a yogi like us and wear our symbols."

Again, Nanak replied with a verse of his song:

Live in the dirt of the world without being blemished by it;
This is the secret for achieving yoga.

24. BANJARA, THE GYPSIES

Our friends walked southward for eighty kilometres and put up just outside the village of Tanda. Most of its inhabitants were the Banjara, gypsies. On their horses and mules, they transported rice grown in the wet Terai region and sold it to people on the plains. The Hindus considered them "impure" outcaste like the untouchables. In India they did not have the right to settle anywhere.

On that day, the Banjaras were celebrating the birth of a son in one of the families. Mardana, always very curious, did not dare to ask Nanak for permission to go there. When night fell, Mardana became very hungry. From a distance he observed that beggars were being given food. Unable to resist any longer, he asked Nanak, "Master, can I go and offer good wishes to the family and get something to eat?"

Nanak smiled and said, "Mardana, this house has not got a child but an awesome sadness. The child will live only this night and will leave tomorrow. If you wish to go there, go ahead, but do not pass on good wishes to anybody, and return silently."

In the crowd, nobody noticed Mardana, who returned quite depressed. As luck would have it, next day the newborn died. The camp wept with sadness and grief. Seeing this sad scene, Nanak sang a song to comfort them.

Mardana asked Nanak, "How do you explain the death of the newly born?"

"It is God's will."

And they departed.

Endnote: Nanak knew that very few newly born infants survive, especially among poor people.

25. THE YOGI WHO LOST HIS ALTAR

From Tanda for a number of months, Nanak and his companions
followed a long route toward the southeast, through dense forest and vast
uninhabited regions. Kings from Delhi came here to hunt lions and tigers.
The trio took a boat in the River Ghagra and after several days reached

Ajodhya, a sacred Hindu city. Lord Rama, the legendary hero of the
Ramayana epic, was born here. They stayed for a few days and then
continued westward by boat and on foot. They took a boat across the

River Tanas, which, like the Ghagra, descends from the Himalayas. After marching some one hundred kilometers, on the way visiting many cities, like Nizamabad, they reached the city of Prayaga, now called Allahabad. Located at the confluence of two sacred rivers, the Ganges and the Yamuna, the city is very sacred for Hindus even now.

According to Hindu mythology, once upon a time, devas and assuras (gods and demons) stopped fighting each other and formed an alliance to work together to produce amrita (nectar) of immortality. They churned the ocean filled with milk. They had agreed to share the divine nectar. But when the jug of nectar appeared, the demons grabbed it and ran away, chased by the gods. For twelve days and nights (twelve human years) they fought a celestial battle. During the fight drops of divine nectar fell at four places—Prayaga, Hardwar, Ujjain, and Nasik.

A huge collective pilgrimage called Kumbh Mela is held in Prayaga, Hardwar, Nasik, or Ujjain every twelve years. Nanak and his two friends witnessed the Kumbh Mela of Prayaga and the spectacular procession.

The procession starts with Nanga Babas, naked yogis, carrying only rosaries, followed by holy people riding elephants, horses and camels. Some are carried in palanquins and others in chariots drawn by men. All show off their devotion and try to outdo each other with the splendour of their retinue.

At a precise moment they dip in the water at the exact point of the *sangam*, confluence, where water transforms into divine nectar. Hindus are convinced that doing this will wash away their sins and those of their descendants for eighty-eight generations to come.

The Nanga Babas are the first to dip in the water; when they come out, they cover their bodies with ashes. Ordinary pilgrims who have waited patiently go in last. These simple people then visit other sadhus sitting in their tents and offering benedictions in exchange for offerings.

Nanak seemed to have ignored the entire scene of bathers. Many sadhus were astonished, and one of them remarked, "Have you lost your senses? Why don't you purify yourself? You will never have such an occasion again."

"What occasion?" Nanak asked candidly.

"For cleansing all your sins."
Nanak recited:

Purity does not come by bathing;
But by having God in your heart.

A little later, the trio followed the crowd towards the camps of sadhus. Nanak saw a pundit with his body covered with sandal paste, sitting majestically in front of a small altar adorned with figurines of idols. His eyes were closed, but he opened them every time someone placed an offering in front of him.

Nanak was much amused by this scene. He asked, "What do see when you close your eyes?"

"When I'm in the state of *samadhi*, meditation, I see the three worlds, the earth, the heavens and the world below. But I request that you not disturb my meditation."

He closed his eyes again. Nanak thought of giving the pundit a surprise. In a whisper he told Bala to put the altar with its idols behind the pundit. Then Nanak placed an offering in the tin. The pundit opened his eyes again. What a surprise—his altar had disappeared! Fuming with anger, he asked Nanak, "Who has the audacity to steal my altar? I can end his life with one word!"

"Holy man," said Nanak gently, "close your eyes and look for it. Surely you will find it within the boundary of the three worlds."

"Please, don't torment me like this. Tell me where my altar is," the pundit implored.

"The altar is secure behind you. But is your soul secure also? I see that you are an intelligent person, but you debase yourself and cheat people for the love of a few coins. My friend, collect the riches of divine Name and share them with others."

As he did here, Nanak often taught people not to believe blindly. His message to everyone was short: Contemplate God, earn and live honestly, and share with those who are in need.

26. GOLD COIN AND NAILS

From Allahabad, Nanak and his two companions took the old road along the Ganges River to Kashi, now known as Benares or Varanasi. To pass the night, the trio stopped in a village just outside a town. A villager saw Nanak and informed a rich city merchant. The following morning the merchant went to see Nanak. Much impressed by his wisdom, he continued to see him every morning and took him something to eat. He listened to Nanak attentively. One day on his way back the merchant met someone who asked him, "O brother, I see you going to the village every morning. Why? Do you go to some woman there?"

"I go to see a holy person."

"May I come with you to see him?

"But of course."

Next morning the two men took the route together. Near the village boundary the second man was attracted to a woman and other people of wicked character. He was tempted to stay with them, and that is what he did, every day. His family believed that he was going to see Nanak. One day the man confided to the merchant: "I pass my time in vice while you serve some hermit. We will see what you gain from that while I enjoy life's pleasures fully. Today, whoever returns first will wait at this spot. We will return to the town together and compare our experiences."

It happened that on that day the man did not find any of his companions and returned to the meeting place early. Not knowing how to pass the time, he started to dig in the earth. Suddenly he found a gold coin. Quickly he took his knife and dug a deeper hole and found a jar that seemed full. Very excited, he lifted the lid. The jar was full of gold coins. They all turned into coal in front of his eyes!

At the same moment the merchant who had become Nanak's disciple knelt before him and then left. As he stepped out of the hut, he injured his foot on a long sharp thorn. He quickly bandaged his foot but could not put his shoe on. He held the shoe in his hand and walked back. When the other man saw the merchant, he asked, "Why aren't you wearing your shoe?"

"I can't, I was injured by a thorn."

"It is strange, I found a gold coin while I was doing bad deeds, while you, who prayed and listened to the holy man, have been pricked by a thorn and injured. How do you explain all this? Let's go and question your holy man."

The two men appeared before Nanak. The man proudly showed Nanak his gold coin.

"That is good," Nanak said. "The jar was full of gold coins. It was the result of the actions of a good person. But each day your sinful actions have transformed that gold into coal. The coin you are holding is the last one."

Much embarrassed, the man responded, "But this merchant got nothing but suffering."

Nanak replied, "Don't be hasty. He was destined to be crucified with nails. Thanks to his pious deeds there remained only one thorn; the nails have disappeared."

From that day on, the man also became Nanak's disciple, started to act in a virtuous way, and was ever happy.

27. ROBBERS

Kashi was still far. So, our friends started their journey early in the morning. Soon some robbers started to follow them. Their leader said, "These three men look very healthy, not like sadhus. They are wearing quality clothes and talk like educated people. I'm sure they are hiding their treasure."

When Nanak and his companions stopped to rest in the shade of a tree, the robbers encircled them and pointed their swords at them. While Nanak was not troubled, Mardana trembled with fear. When the leader ordered them to hand over their treasure, Nanak asked him with a smile, "Who are you?"

"We are robbers; we are going to kill you."

"Very well," said Nanak. "Would you fulfil one wish before you kill us?"

"What do you want?"

"Look behind you; there is smoke. Can you bring the fire that you'll need to light the pyre when you burn us?"

"I do not know what you are talking about. Kill them!"

But one of the robbers spoke up, "Chief, we have killed many people, but never before has anyone asked with a smile that we kill them. Anyway, they cannot escape from us."

The leader ordered two of his men to bring the fire. When the two reached the spot, they were greatly surprised. They saw the smoke rising from a funeral pyre. In the smoky mist they saw two silhouettes fighting each other. The startled robbers asked, "Who are you? Why are you fighting?"

"I am the Angel of Death. God has sent me to fetch this man, who has just died. I will take him to the deepest part of hell. But this Heaven's Angel has suddenly appeared out of nowhere. He is preventing me from completing my task."

Then Heaven's Angel responded, "This man was a great sinner. I too would have pushed him towards hell's gate. But the smoke of this pyre caught the attention of Nanak, the man you want to kill. Thanks to him, this man will go to heaven."

The two robbers turned around, ran back, and fell at Nanak's feet, ignoring their leader.

"What has happened to you?" the leader shouted.

They told him what they had witnessed and said, "This man is not just a sadhu. He is truly a holy man. Seek his forgiveness."

All the robbers knelt down before Nanak. "We are sinners. We have committed abominable crimes. Forgive us."

Nanak showed mercy and spoke with love, "You will be pardoned only if you start earning an honest living. Go and distribute among the poor all that you have robbed and share with them what you will earn in the future."

28. PUNDITS OF VARANASI

At last Nanak, Bala, and Mardana reached Kashi. They stayed about two kilometres from the sacred Ganges. Nanak already knew that this city was famous for being the abode of the god Shiva. Even today, Hindus strongly believe that to die here is an express route to paradise. The travellers saw countless pilgrims looking for their final salvation.

There were an equal number of pundits, the wise and learned men, especially Brahmins, well versed in philosophy. They conversed with each other and claimed that they were the unique masters of all knowledge and religion.

Nanak's neighbour was a Brahmin named Ganga Ram. He was much impressed by Nanak. They agreed that Nanak should preach in public starting the next day. But Nanak's message irritated most of the other Brahmins.

On the bank of the Ganges Nanak saw many pundits absorbed in reading books in front of their disciples. Many more, with their faces and bodies smeared with ashes from the cremation ground, were meditating. On seeing Nanak, some of them would approach him and ask him what he was doing there. One morning a Brahmin named Chatar Das, returning from the ritual of purifying himself in the Ganges, saw Nanak singing with Mardana and Ganga Ram. He noticed immediately that Nanak was not a Brahmin. Standing in front of Nanak, he said, "You talk as though you have limitless knowledge. Have you read the Vedas and Sastras?"

Nanak calmly replied by reciting:

One may read cartloads of books,
With caravan-loads of books to follow;
One may study boatloads of volumes,
And file them in the cellars;
One may spend years and months solely in reading,

Until the last breath of life;
But I believe that only contemplative life matters;
All else is fret and fever that serves to glorify the ego.

Chatar Das, vexed by this confrontation, fired back with a question: "Are you saying that studying Vedas and Sastras is a waste of time?"

Nanak replied, "It's useless to study if their teachings are not put into practice. It's like the light of a lighthouse engulfed in darkness. Light is useful to show the way to a person who is lost."

"O sadhu, you don't even have your idol, nor basil-wood rosary, nor a symbol on your forehead painted with sandalwood. How can you be truly religious? What level of spirituality have you attained?"

Nanak said, "Mardana, play the melody of spring."

O Brahmin, make the stone idol of Vishnu the prayer;
Your basil-wood rosary your conduct.

The two men continued to debate for a long time. At last, Chatar Das admitted that Nanak was a man of God.

The orthodox Hindus have invented numerous rituals. The most important, practiced even today, is that of purity. One day a Brahmin invited Nanak for dinner. "One must strictly observe the code of purity in cooking and eating," said the Brahmin.

Before entering his house, he looked around to see if there was some untouchable person around. Then he guided Nanak to his kitchen, justifying everything. "You see, I've constructed the hearth with soil I dug with my own hands. I plastered it with sacred cow dung. The firewood I washed with water of the Ganges. You have seen that I bathed in the waters of the Ganges; I am pure."

He cooked the food with utmost care and put the dish in front of Nanak, who said, "I can't eat this impure food."

The Brahmin was stupefied. "What do you think purity is?"

"Only the spirit that remains concentrated on God is pure. Moreover, there is nothing and there is no place that does not hold living things. The cow dung and the firewood are full of worms."

The Brahmin suddenly saw the spiritual light and changed his thinking completely.

29. GAYA THE DEVIL

Nanak left Kashi after showing the right path to many pundits. From the Ganges Nanak's route turned towards the southwest. It is said that on the way Nanak met Kabir, who was going to Kashi to meet him. Kabir was a simple weaver and a formidable mystic poet, a father of modern spirituality. For many days the two great souls exchanged ideas and experiences. It is believed that Kabir presented his songs to Nanak, who took very good care of them. These songs now form one-eighth of the holy book of the Sikhs, *Adi Granth*.

Forty-five kilometres from the place they met, Nanak stopped at Chandrauli. The village chief, Hari Das, greatly appreciated Nanak's message of humility and charity. The three visited Gaya, the place where Buddha had attained spiritual illumination two thousand years earlier. Nanak was sitting on the bank of the River Phalgu. Soon a group of pundits surrounded him reciting sacred texts. Their leader offered to help Nanak. "This is Vishnu's sacred place. Thousands of people come here to save their dead ancestors so that they can be liberated and enter paradise. Only we know the correct ritual. We can do that for the three of you."

"What should I do?" Nanak asked.

"First light a lamp in the holy Vishnu pad temple, at the feet of Vishnu. Then we'll take charge."

"Why at the feet of Vishnu?" Nanak asked.

These priests did not want people to follow Buddha's teachings. They were bent on degrading him. One of the priests answered Nanak, "Gaya is the old name of the angel of death or devil. Once the devil decided to change his life. He started to meditate and remained in a meditative state for many years. Finally, Vishnu, who was very happy with Gaya, appeared before him and asked, 'What is your desire?'

"'Give me a power that will keep anyone who sees me from going to hell,' replied the devil.

"'Your request is too easy to grant,' Vishnu said. "'Anyone who simply looks at my feet will not go to hell.' And Vishnu disappeared."

Nanak listened to this story attentively. But when he saw the great temple of Vishnu pad, "Vishnu's feet", he decided not to follow the advice of the priests. Nanak said, "I have already lit a divine lamp in my heart for myself and my ancestors. My ritual is to remove the darkness of ignorance. This ignorance is the true hell. Those who have lit the lamp of divine knowledge are liberated."

30. THE JEWELLER

From Gaya, the trio trekked northward to join the Ganges River again at Patliputra, now called Patna. Three centuries before Jesus Christ, this city was the capital of Emperor Asoka the Great. He had conquered nearly the whole of India and then converted to Buddhism. The legend is that Buddha had foretold these events two centuries earlier. Nanak saw only the ruins of this city. He then crossed the river and entered the large city of Hajipur. Before they could even settle down, Mardana complained, "O Master, I'm hungry. I can't sleep on an empty stomach."

"Go to the jewellers' street; you'll find plenty to eat."

Mardana begged for food at many houses. One jeweller placed three paisa coins in his hand. Mardana, quite disappointed, went to the house of another jeweller, who was eating his meal. That jeweller told his accountant, Adarka, to deal with the beggar. Seeing poor hungry Mardana, Adarka invited him in and took him to the jeweller, whose name was Salis Rai. He was a generous and pious person. He fed Mardana to his fill and then gave him some money and food for his companions. Mardana returned to Nanak looking very happy. "Why have you brought this money? Go back and return it!"

When Mardana returned the money, Salis was greatly impressed and said, "This is unusual. I want to meet your master. Take me to him. Here, take some more food with you."

Salis bowed before Nanak and said, "Your disciple is a treasure. What is your secret? Teach me also."

31. THE SORCERESS QUEEN OF KAMROOP

From Patna, Nanak and his companions had to cross many rivers flowing from the Himalayas. Passing through the towns of Munghir, Karagola, and Mald, they reached the confluence of the Ganges with the River Brahmaputra. This is a much bigger river, several kilometres wide. After visiting Dacca, they took a boat on the Brahmaputra and sailed upstream, northward and then to the east, towards the land of Assam. The boat advanced very slowly. They visited many towns, in particular Gauhati, one of the most sacred places for Hindus. A little farther on they disembarked and walked to the Kaurou region, which was inhabited by Kochi tribes with strange customs. One track took them to the town of Kamroop. Nanak and Bala camped a little outside the town while Mardana, always hungry, could not resist going to look for food. Before he left, Nanak warned him, "A strange queen rules over this country. Be careful!"

The queen's name was Noorshah. She practiced *tantra*, a type of black magic, and worshipped the goddess Kamakhya, to whom people offered human sacrifices. She kept control over all her people. Many inhabitants also practiced black magic. But Noorshah was the most powerful of them all.

Mardana walked a short distance and came to a house. In front of the house he saw three quite happy-looking women. One of them asked him, "Why have you come to our village?"

Mardana replied in the Punjabi language. They could not understand a word of what he said. But they were greatly amused by the way he behaved and by the clothes he wore. Merrily mocking him, one of them flicked her fingers and turned him into a ram. Another tied a cord around his neck, and he found himself on four legs, bleating like a real ram. The three women laughed and clapped their hands as they danced joyously around poor Mardana.

After waiting quite a while, Nanak said to Bala, "It's been some time and Mardana has not returned. Surely, he has encountered some misfortune. Come, let's go look for him."

Soon they met a woman coming out of the house with a water pot on her head. Nanak asked her, "Have you by chance seen one of our companions?"

"No, I haven't. You can search my house."

When Nanak entered the enclosure, Mardana started to bleat, "Baa, baa!"

One of the witches pointed at Nanak and shrieked, "Look at that one! I'm going to make him bark like a dog!"

Not knowing what to make of this nonsense, Nanak said, "You, yourself will take the form of what you are thinking."

And at once the woman changed into a bitch. Nanak recited a prayer and the cord around Mardana's neck broke and fell off. Then he turned to Mardana and said, "Repeat after me: 'God is wonderful!'"

At the same time, Nanak pronounced some mysterious words that broke the magic and returned Mardana to human form.

Meanwhile, the second witch, rushed towards Bala and cast a spell on him. But suddenly she froze and was stuck there like a statue, unable to move.

The third woman tried to free her companion, but she too was petrified on the spot, with the water pot cemented solidly to her head.

Evidently, someone ran to Noorshah and told her what had happened.

Livid, the queen ordered all the witches in the city to follow her. Some flew on their brooms, others on their antelopes. All gathered at the spot, beating drums and cursing Nanak. But all their spells had no effect. They tried all their magic tricks and used all their powers but could not liberate the three women. For the first time, the sorceress queen's magic and the magic of her witches turned out to be useless.

Noorshah was terrified by Nanak's powers. She placed a great heap of gold and jewels at Nanak's feet and begged him to teach her his magic. Nanak told her, "First, take away all these offerings. Now listen: the only true treasure is the word of God, whose power is to heal hearts and grant everlasting peace."

This was the first time the poor queen had met a master like Nanak. She understood that this was her great good fortune and lamented, "Kindly forgive me. I am wrong. I believed that it was right to follow my tribal traditions. Please free my sisters and show us the right path."

"In fact, that's why I have come here," Nanak revealed. Then he reanimated the three women and said, "God's light shines in full splendour when our thinking converges towards him. Suffering disappears when we stop doing bad things."

The entire town of Kamroop was liberated from the black magic. Praises of God replaced all the spells and charms. After a few days, Nanak and his companions left that town, leaving behind them the aura of calm.

32. THE OGRE'S HOT CAULDRON

This time, Nanak chose to walk along the River Brahmaputra. The three comrades visited many villages and met all kinds of people. As they entered one village, the villagers began to laugh at them, taunted them, and chased them away.

"Go away, there is no place for gypsies here."

Nanak responded, "May the inhabitants of this village flourish here."

A little farther along the three men approached another village. The villagers welcomed them lovingly and shared food with them. Next morning as he left the village, Nanak said, "May this village be uprooted and dispersed."

Later Mardana could not resist asking Nanak, "Master, why did you bless those who chased us away and curse those who honoured and served us so well?"

"The people of the first village will keep their meanness and vice there in their village, but those of the second village will spread their generosity and goodness throughout the whole world."

After a few days of trekking farther east along the River Brahmaputra they reached the town of Golaghat at the confluence with the River Thanasi, which flowed from the Naga Mountains in the south. Our three friends turned south and followed the Dhanasri valley, which was covered with dense forest. In Golaghat someone had warned them, "You must not go there. It's dangerous."

"We have crossed India and encountered thousands of people of all kinds; God has always protected us," Nanak replied.

Nevertheless, the villagers alerted them: "This valley is inhabited by the Nagas. They are cannibals. They catch and sacrifice men, women and children of other villages and eat them. Their chief is Kauda. He is huge and ferocious, like an ogre. Surely they will eat you."

Nanak wanted to show Kauda and his tribe how to live in a correct and healthy way. They walked through this difficult region for many days until they reached the foot of a hill. There Mardana stopped suddenly and whispered, "I hear someone walking behind the trees. Someone is tracking us."

He began to tremble with fear.

"It's your imagination. There's nobody here," Nanak assured him.

Their journey was long and very tiring. Mardana was hungry and Nanak was well aware of it.

"See, there is smoke rising from the village in front of us. Go look for something to eat there," Nanak told him. Mardana left.

They were indeed being followed by Naga savages. One of the Naga ran to inform Kauda, the village chief, that the three men were just outside the village. The villagers were very happy that they would not have to hunt that day; their prey was coming towards them. Mardana reached a clearing in the forest. He saw the savages dancing around an enormous cauldron suspended over a huge fire. But before he could escape, four very strong men caught him from behind. They bound him with a rope and presented him to Kauda.

"I was waiting. What luck! Today we'll have plenty to eat." Kauda laughed loudly, showing his big teeth. "Add more wood to the fire. Make the water boil quickly," he ordered. Frightened to death, Mardana closed his eyes, prayed to God and thought of Nanak.

"Only you can save me."

Kauda touched the water in the cauldron. He was astonished—the water was not very hot.

"Add more wood," he ordered.

Nanak and Bala were awaiting Mardana's return. They began to worry. "I wonder what has happened to Mardana. Let's go see," Nanak said.

And what did they see from the edge of the clearing? They saw the savages holding Mardana and preparing to throw him in the cauldron. Nanak raised his hand, closed his eyes and contemplated God. When he opened his eyes, he saw Mardana standing in the cauldron. The water was still not hot. Kauda was furious. Nanak and Bala were soon captured as well and dragged towards the fire. Kauda seized Nanak and threw him into the flames. But Nanak walked out of the fire as though nothing had happened. He looked into Kauda's eyes and smiled graciously. Kauda understood that he was facing a saintly person of God. He and his people fell to their knees at Nanak's feet.

Imagine how relieved Mardana felt! He emerged from the cauldron unscathed and thanked his master for saving him.

Nanak said, "Brother Kauda, rise. Give up your sinful life. Do not harm anyone around you. Be benevolent and merciful."

Nanak stayed with the tribe for many days and taught them God's word: "Earn your living by honest work, share it with the poor and contemplate God. Kauda, command your people to do the same, and lead them on the right path."

Kauda promised to follow Nanak's advice.

33. MONSTER FISH AND EVENING WORSHIP

Nanak and his friends trekked back along the River Dhanasri to Brahmaputra. There they boarded a boat to the city of Gauhati. Then they took a rough southerly route that passed through the beautiful countryside of Shillong and Sylhet. First a boat on the Surma River and then a long march took them to the town of Agartala. Most of the people of this region were Muslims. Nanak met and talked with many Sufi holy men.

It is difficult to imagine how many months they walked in those times, when the routes were not well marked. Even now, there are many people who think that Nanak was a super magician, that he could fly at the speed of light from one place to another and even teleport himself— he had simply to visualize a destination, no matter how far, and abracadabra! he appeared at that place!

Legend also has it that the three travellers descended to the port of Chittagong on the Bay of Bengal. There Nanak saw an enormous fish, much bigger than a whale, in fact many kilometres long. But Bala and Mardana did not notice anything.

"Let's go up to it," Nanak said, "and then continue walking." After a little while Nanak asked his companions, "Do you sense something?"

"Master, I do not understand anything. Only you can enlighten us."

"You haven't even noticed that for many hours we have been walking on the back of a fish, and we have passed an entire night!"

At last, they reached the head of the fish. Frightened by its cavernous mouth, Mardana closed his eyes and whispered, "O master, may Allah save me!"

The fish turned its head and spoke to Nanak: "I thank you from the bottom of my heart. You have freed me from this life."

"But who are you?" Nanak asked. "What happened to you?"

"A long time ago I was a king's attendant. One day he sent me to do some work. I did it, but with much anger inside me. The king noticed, and said, 'You work like a fish wriggling out of water.' In fact, he cast a charm on me that changed me into a fish. Meeting you has liberated me from this curse."

As soon our friends left, the fish disappeared into the country of gods. Saved from the monster, Mardana took a deep breath of relief.

This time they boarded a boat and entered the vast delta of the Ganges-Brahmaputra. After resting in the village of Dhaka, they reached the other side of the delta. Passing through Kolkata, they followed the east coast for many long days and stopped in the port city of Cuttack. News of their coming had reached the king ahead of them.

He came to listen to Nanak's teachings, and the news of this incident reached the ear of a pundit. He was the chief priest of the temple of Jagannath, not far from Puri, another very sacred city of Hindus. The pundit was furious. In his estimation, if there existed a greatest scholar of logic, religion and mathematics, then it was he himself. He could not bear the thought that the king had gone to see a rival, an insignificant sadhu like Nanak.

At Puri the deep blue sea and the sky merged harmoniously with the earth. This city attracted many yogis and holy men. Chaitainya, one of the first bhaktas, Hindu Sufi lovers of God, also happened to be in Puri when Nanak arrived there.

Nanak suggested to Bala and Mardana, "This afternoon we will visit the famous temple of Jagannath."

"How is this temple different from all those we have already seen?" asked Bala.

"This temple is dedicated to Jagannath, the guardian of the universe. The evening worship here is well known in the Hindu world."

There they encountered the proud grand priest. Nanak was highly impressed by his discourse. At the end the pundit proposed, "Would you like to participate in the evening worship?"

"With great pleasure," Nanak replied.

Exactly when the sun disappeared behind the sea, the great pundit and a following of other priests and pilgrims gathered in the temple. The sound of bells could be heard far away. Preparations for the worship of Jagannath progressed in the customary manner. Suddenly, the conches blared, the incense was lit, bells chimed, and oil lamps lit up the scene. Bala and Mardana were tempted to join the crowd, but Nanak continued to sit under a tree, observing the agitation with much curiosity. He watched the colourful sunset reflected on the waves of the sea, and then the moon and the stars twinkling in the sky. He breathed in the air, scented with the fragrance of sandalwood. Closing his eyes, he found perfect peace in the nature around him. Bala and Mardana had to stay with him.

The worship ended. The grand priest came out and noticed that Nanak was sitting under the tree. Quite annoyed, he asked, "What happened to you? Why didn't you participate in the worship of God Jagannath, the guardian of the universe?"

"Where can he be found?" Nanak questioned in return.

"Are you blind? Don't you see the majestic statue standing before your eyes?"

Nanak looked at his interlocutor with affection. "Am I really blind? Tell me, how can a simple wooden statue represent the God of the universe, he who is beyond human imagination, he who is immeasurable, he who pervades everything?"

"Be careful what you say!" many people shouted angrily at Nanak.

But Nanak calmed them and continued, "What I have said is the truth. The lord of the universe does not reside in wooden statues carved by artisans but manifests in the heart of each one of us."

The pundit interrupted him, "But where are your candles, pearls, incense? How can you worship him?"

Nanak signalled to Mardana, "Play the rebab, Mardana!" Then he pointed towards the sky and sang:

The vast sky is the tray;
In it, the sun and the moon are the lamps,
And the celestial stars are like pearls.
The sandalwood-scented wind from the Malai hills is the incense,
It sways like a whisk;
All of plant life supplies sacred flowers for You, O Light.
What beauty unfurls in nature, the evening worship that wipes out fear!
Without the drum beater, the drum resonates with the rhythm of Name.

The crowd fell silent in admiration. Even those who had doubted the most stopped resisting and wisely submitted to the words coming from Nanak's mouth. And in their minds, they saw a new light.

Endnote: The "monster fish" was a long sand bar that often formed and disappeared in the Ganges Delta.

34. NANAK WALKS ON WATER AND GOES TO SRI LANKA

Sri Lanka is a large island that seems to be suspended like a diamond from the tip of southern India. Its former name is Sangladeep, the island of the Sangla people. Its northeast part, inhabited by the Tamils, was ruled by Raja Shiv Nabh, a very generous king. All his people respected him.

Once, a merchant from Punjab named Mansukh went to Sri Lanka to start a business. One thing led to another, and he set up a big shop. He often spoke to clients about his master, a wise man full of love. You must have already guessed: this wise man was Nanak.

Soon, Mansukh's stories reached the ears of the Raja.

"This merchant does not observe the day of fasting," the Raja's Minister reported. "Despite your Majesty's instructions, he doesn't wear Siva's symbol on his forehead, or worship him."

"Bring me this person," ordered the Raja.

Kneeling before the Raja, Mansukh told him about the teachings of Nanak and recited his poems.

"These words are sublime," said the Raja, fascinated. "How can I too meet your master?"

"If your heart is pure and you pray to see him, Nanak will not fail to grant your wish," replied Mansukh.

From that day, every morning, Raja prayed so that Nanak would reveal himself to him. He was convinced that one day Nanak would come. So, he lovingly planted some trees that would provide shade for the wise man. He knew that Nanak loved nature.

Mansukh returned to Punjab but found no sign of Nanak. That saddened the Raja. Many people pretending to be saints came and sat down under the grove of trees. But they were all imposters. Days, months and years passed without a trace of Nanak. Shiv Nabh gradually lost all hope and neglected the trees. One by one, the trees began to lose their leaves before drying out completely.

Legend has it that Nanak had actually heard Raja's prayers. Seven years had passed since Nanak, Bala and Mardana left their village. We know their route across the plains, high mountains and thick forests. They traversed rivers large and small, and often walked in the hot sun and through torrential rainstorms and fierce winds. But we do not know the exact dates of their visit to each place.

After seeing Puri, they walked for several months and reached Chennai. Southern India has so many cultural and religious sites that they could not visit them all. Then, passing through Guntur, Nanak decided to walk some eighty kilometres inland from the coast and visited 200 Buddhist, Hindu and Jain temples in Kanchipuram. Monks of various spiritual beliefs came to know in advance of the arrival of a holy man from the North. They welcomed Nanak and spoke with him until they were all satisfied.

A Jain monk asked him: "You who eat food that grows in the ground, drink fresh water and, in this way, consume living beings—how can you be a spiritual master?"

Here are a few lines from a long song that Nanak sang describing how some sects of Jains lived:

They have their head-hair plucked, and drink filthy water;
They beg daily and eat leftovers others have thrown away;
They spread their own excrement, inhaling its foul smell through the mouth;
Clean water frightens them;
They have abandoned the lifestyle of their parents;
They remain filthy day and night;
They wander without giving charity, or bathing;
Their shaved heads are covered with ashes.

Look at a map of India to see the cities our friends visited. Trivanmalai, the starting point of roads in all directions, looked beautiful with its magnificent temple of Siva and his wife Parvathi. They stopped near Trichnapalli and stayed in the Vishnu temple called Sri Rangam, between the rivers Kaveri and Kolerun. It is here that two men, Saido and Siho, joined them, bringing news from Punjab.

"Your families want you to return home. Nanak, your parents are quite old and cannot support the family. Your sons have grown up. They need their father," reported the two messengers.

Nanak replied, "We have an important appointment. For quite some time, I sense that someone is calling me in Sri Lanka. After that, we'll return to Punjab."

A boat on the Kaveri brought them to the major port city of Nagappattinam. Standing on the seashore, the trio were looking towards the south when Nanak remarked, "This blue ocean is wide and deep. There is no boat to take us. Raja is waiting for me. I have to meet him. But how to cross the ocean?"

Saido and Siho replied, "At your command the stones can float." And Nanak recited a verse:

Ek onkar, satnaam, karta purkh, nirbhau, nirvair, akal murat, adjouni sai bhen. Gur prasad.
(One Supreme Being, all-pervading. Eternal truth that enfolds all. Ultimate creative-reality; without fear and hate. Timeless image, not incarnated, self-existent, Gracious Enlightener-Guru.)

"Whoever recites these words can cross the ocean. Follow me."

What joy! The five travellers closed their eyes and marched in single file across the sea. Surely you have realized that this is only a legend. Our friends actually boarded a ship and travelled for several days to get to Trincomalee, a major port on the East coast of Sri Lanka. A little farther lies Matiakalam, the capital where the Raja lived. But this fascinating legend lives on.

They went directly to the grove of trees that the Raja had planted, and hardly were they seated when the trees found all their beauty: dry leaves turned green, and flowers bloomed fresh. Even fruit appeared to be fully ripe. The news of this miracle spread like wildfire. But the Raja, who had already dealt with many imposters, was not at all impressed. In order to verify that his host truly was Nanak, he ordered two of his most beautiful dancers to go to the grove and seduce Nanak. Dressed lightly and in stunning makeup, proud of their beauty and the charm of their music, the girls entered the garden, sure of their success.

However, the moment they arrived, an indescribable calm took hold of their minds. They approached Nanak with humility and knelt before him. Then they sat down respectfully at a distance, amazed at Nanak's song accompanied by soft music played by Mardana on the rebab.

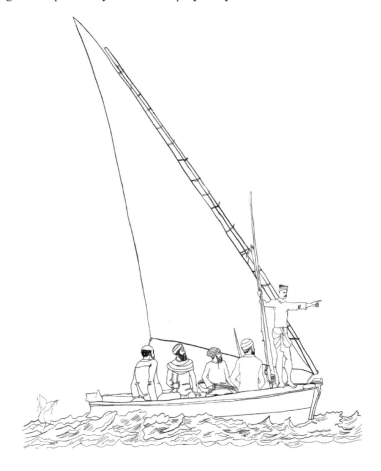

Upon learning that his dancers had failed, Raja Shiv Nabh was struck with remorse and the need to repent for testing Nanak. Without waiting, he walked straightaway to his long-neglected grove.

When he saw Nanak, he was filled with joy and fell at his feet

"Bless me with your grace," he said, "and accept me. I have waited for you for many years."

"I came because of your devotion. I knew you were waiting," said Nanak, embracing the Raja.

Little by little, the inhabitants of the city also began to gather under the grove. The king and his people visited Nanak and his companions regularly. The Raja became Nanak's disciple. After a long stay, Nanak wanted to take leave and continue his journey. To soften their sadness, the Raja and his queen, Chandrakla, proposed, "O master, have dinner with us before you leave."

Remember that the Raja had tested Nanak in several ways before he acknowledged Nanak's true identity. Now it was Nanak's turn to test the Raja.

"Today, I am fasting," replied Nanak.

"How will we be forgiven?" lamented the Raja. Serving a meal to a saintly person is a Hindu tradition for obtaining salvation.

"If you have human flesh, I can have lunch," said Nanak.

"I have a lot of men."

"O Raja, I want to have one who is son of a king and twelve years old."

Raja inquired around, "Which king has a son?"

The queen replied, "No king will give you his son. First, you have to fight him and win the battle. Our own son is twelve years old."

Raja looked at his son and said, "My son, your body will serve the master well. What is your wish?"

The son replied, "I offer my body with joy."

But Raja interrupted him, "The prince married only seven days ago. We must find out if his wife agrees."

The Raja went to see the princess. "Can your husband's body be used to serve our spiritual master?"

The princess replied without hesitation, "O father, his body as well as my becoming a widow are the best offerings we can make to the master."

Returning to Nanak, the Raja declared, "Sire, this boy is yours."

"He is of no use to me like this. The queen should hold his arms and the princess hold his legs, and then you cut a piece of his flesh and offer it to me."

The Raja did what Nanak had asked him and laid before him a plate of cooked meat. When Nanak lifted a piece of meat to his mouth, he told the Raja, his queen and their daughter-in-law to close their eyes and repeat "O wonderful Illuminator." When the three opened their eyes, they were… four! The son was among them, alive and well, but Nanak had disappeared. The Raja had passed Nanak's test.

For one whole year our friends visited the rest of the island, including the kingdom of Dharamaprakarmabahu, ruled by the king of the Sangla people in Kotte, near Colombo. Nanak returned to Matiakalam. The Raja and his family were immensely pleased to see him again. Nanak then went to Anuradhapura, where he talked with Buddhist monks and started his return journey. They took a boat from Mannar to cross the strait and regained India at the port of Rameshwar.

35. LAND OF DEMONS

On the long journey from Sri Lanka, our friends met people of all kinds, good and bad. Once, on an island, their road was suddenly traversed by hundreds of deer, followed by a line of boars, which were pursued by dogs, then hunters on horses, and finally the king, whose name was Madhurbain. Mardana, hungry as usual, had to wait long to look for food in the city. When Mardana saw the king in his way, he said angrily: "Have you no eyes? Don't you know who we are?"

Knowing that his friend could not bear to be hungry for long, Bala quickly changed the tone of his voice and addressed the king very courteously, "We have come from afar, and we do not know anyone here."

"Who are you?" the king asked.

"Nanak is my master. Mardana and I, Bala, accompany him. We are from Punjab."

The king, who had already been told of Nanak's arrival, got down from his horse and knelt respectfully before Nanak. He invited him and his friends to his palace, where they stayed a few days.

Then our three friends crossed a mountainous country and the forest of Gandhar. Its king, Devloot, was a demon. The three stopped in a beautiful clearing. Tired, Mardana complained, "It's been three days. We haven't eaten anything. Bala and you, you don't need to eat. But I am very hungry. I can't go on."

"You see the building ahead? Its master is a demon like Kauda. Remember, I saved you when Kauda threw you into a pot of boiling water. Go and ask him for food and drink," said Nanak.

"I will never enter this cursed town."

"If you don't go, you're going to die of hunger. You don't really have a choice."

"Why do you want me to be devoured by demons? Better kill me."

They were joking like this when king Devloot, accompanied on a hunting trip by a horde of terrible demons, stopped and stood in front of our three friends. Seeing their huge bodies, their very dark skin, their long teeth, their nostrils and cavernous mouths, red bloodshot eyes and necklaces of bones, Mardana choked and cried, "Well, now we are really dead! Do something before they kill us."

"My dear Mardana, think of God in your heart, calm down and see how the game is played," Nanak advised him.

When he saw them, Devloot rubbed his hands and grinned gleefully: "It's been a long time since I have eaten human flesh. Go and catch the three men," he ordered.

Three demons approached our friends, but suddenly the demons became blind and did not know where to go. Unable to do anything, they turned back and immediately they could see.

"Why do you not obey me?" demanded Devloot.

Trembling, they reported what had happened. The king sent three other demons, who ran towards our friends. But as soon as they approached them, they too became blind.

"O king, we too have been blinded and regained our sight when we turned around."

The demon king could make no sense of this. He sent seven teams of demons, one after another, but none of them were able to catch the three men. He turned to his Minister for advice.

"O king, this person seems to be charmed. With your permission I'd like to go meet him."

Reciting some prayer, the Minister approached Nanak. He knelt before Nanak and quietly asked, "What is your name?"

"I am Nanak."

"And where are you from?"

"We are from Punjab, but the world is our home and we live according to the will of God."

The Minister informed Devloot, "God's avatar himself has come to pardon us. You better go talk to him."

But Devloot retorted, "I want my human flesh. I do not need your advice."

He ordered all the demons to follow him, and all walked sternly towards our friends. As they came near, all became blind except for the Minister. Then Devloot admitted, "You were right, Minister. Would he forgive me and release me so I can see?"

The Minister knew that his king's heart had been purified and that he wanted to be saved. He begged Nanak, "O master, show yourself to the king."

"He can open his eyes now," said Nanak.

When he opened his eyes, Devloot found himself standing before Nanak.

"Forgive me, master. Please accept my invitation to stay in our village," pleaded Devloot.

Mardana leaped with joy. They lived with the villagers for several days. Nanak's teachings changed the people's way of life completely. They ceased to be cannibals and instead became vegetarian. They formed a habit of meeting morning and evening to meditate and praise God.

36. THE GIGANTIC OGRE

The day came for the three to leave the kingdom of Devloot and continue their journey. They soon found themselves in the middle of a magnificent forest with trees of all kinds bedecked with juicy fruit. Suddenly, a group of wild men leaped across their path. They were naked, with frightening faces, and they were acting like animals. The group paused for a moment and looked at the three travellers. Then they all left except for one, who stood and peered intently at our three friends. Very frightened, Mardana asked, "Who is this? I'm scared!"

"Don't be afraid, Mardana. They are people of the woods."

"Ask him why he's watching us like this."

"Who are you?" asked Bala.

The man of the woods howled like an animal. Bala asked Nanak, "Why doesn't he talk like us?"

"They are just like that, wild. They have not yet learned to speak."

This man of the woods began to pick fruit. He placed it on the trail very close to them and then ran away to rejoin his group.

Mardana, hungry as usual, ate the fruit and satisfied his desire. Then they continued their journey.

After marching for a few days, they found themselves in the middle of another forest that was just as charming. Mardana had never seen fruit so big and flowers so beautiful. But the forest seemed deserted—no animals or birds, just silence. After a brief rest, Mardana could not contain himself and asked Nanak, "I'm hungry. If you'll excuse me, could I pick some fruit?"

"Be patient, Mardana. I do not see any birds or other animals. It's a bad sign."

"You're strange," said Mardana. "When there are good things to eat, you forbid me. It appears that you would like me to die of hunger. I sense that my grave will be here," Mardana grumbled. Muttering, he walked

117

away to pick fruit. The fruit looked so good that he quickly began to eat, forgetting everything else. Without the slightest noise a gigantic ogre, big as a mountain, appeared behind him. His arms were at least three kilometres long. On his head were two large horns the size of palm trees. His nostrils were like enormous caves. You won't believe me, but this giant swallowed Mardana whole, as if he were just an egg. From the ogre's belly Mardana started to call Nanak. He regretted bitterly not listening to his master's advice and having spoken unkindly. He meditated and prayed hard so that Nanak would save him as he had done so many times before.

Nanak got up, asked Bala to stay, and hurried off to save Mardana. When the giant saw Nanak, he swallowed Nanak whole as well. Inside the ogre's belly Nanak found Mardana and encouraged him not to lose hope. Suddenly, Nanak's body began to inflate like a balloon. The ogre's belly swelled so much that he fell to the ground, crushing many trees under him. The fall caused his stomach to burst, and our two friends walked out unharmed.

They saw the ogre's soul leave his body and rise towards the sky. Then a rain of flowers fell upon them. The ogre turned into a handsome man. He knelt before Nanak and said, "O master, thank you for saving me, a sinner."

At that moment, Bala joined them and asked, "Who is this man?"

"I'll let him answer you," replied Nanak.

The ogre who had become a man spoke. "Once I was the cook of King Janak. One day I was cooking for a big religious festival. A craving overtook me, and I tasted the food before serving it to the holy men. Someone told the king what I had done. He declared the food to be impure and ordered that it be thrown in the river. He condemned me and transformed me into an ogre. I devoured all the animals of the forest. O master, after so many years you have finally freed me." He knelt before Nanak and with a flash flew off to heaven.

"How is it that this sinner who has devoured all the birds and other animals deserves to go to heaven?" asked Bala.

"In his early life he served the holy men and meditated on the name of God. This is the result of his generosity."

Endnote: This story was invented by priests to convince uneducated people that feeding the priests was a charitable act that would take them to heaven.

37. THE RICH BANKER

Nanak and his companions were keen to return to Punjab quickly. The journey ahead was still five thousand kilometres. Can you imagine walking in sweltering heat, through rainforests infested with wild animals? They visited countless Hindu temples in Trivandrum, the land of Kerala, the Nilgiri hills, and Palghat on the Kaveri River. Then they crossed the vast, dry Deccan plateau in the burning sun. They stopped to rest at Nanded on the Godavari River. After crossing two rivers, the Tapti and the Narmada, they reached Baroach, a large port city in the west, on the Arabian Sea coast. To satisfy Mardana, they headed northwest to the land of Gujarat to see the sacred Hindu temples of Somnath and Dwarka. These temples were sumptuously rich. Finally, they turned eastward and took the trade route that brought them to the famous Rocks of Girnar near Junagarh, then to the cities of Ahmedabad and Ujjain, Pushkar, and Jaipur-Amber in the middle of the Rajasthan Desert. At Mathura on the River Yamuna, where the God Krishna is supposed have lived, they visited the forest of Brindaban. Here the young Krishna used to play with his girlfriends, who looked after the herds of cows.

Not far from Delhi, the group reached a large town. They camped on the bank of the River Yamuna. Here our friends met a banker who invited them to stay in his big house. He was very rich and powerful and had a good heart. He had built a dharamsala, a hostel that welcomed and lodged pilgrims. Nanak declined his offer, saying that he had already been invited elsewhere. Hardly had he finished speaking when a poor goldsmith approached and said to Nanak, "Holy traveller, please stay with me and bless my simple house. I can't offer you anything other than my humble services and my love."

Surely Nanak was expecting this. He got up, followed by Bala and Mardana, and accompanied the goldsmith. The banker was surprised.

They arrived at a small hut. It had two rooms without any furniture. One room was given to the guests. The goldsmith's wife brought a large container of water, and the goldsmith began tenderly to wash Nanak's feet. Then he served his guests a simple meal lovingly prepared.

The banker, who lived nearby in a luxurious house, could not ease his mind knowing that Nanak was in the vicinity. Finally, he approached the hut and saw Nanak resting on the ground.

"You'd be much more comfortable in my house," he could not help pointing out.

"Why? Do you think I feel less comfortable here?" replied the guru. "It is to those who deny themselves worldly things that God gives his grace. I am looking for the company of God lovers so that I too can attain God's grace."

The banker walked away pensively, Nanak's words echoing in his ears. Next morning, he came back.

"I have a favour to ask of you," said Nanak.

"I am at your service," replied the banker, pleased to be useful to the holy man.

"Actually, I don't really need anything. As a banker, your job is to deposit and safeguard valuable things. Look, here is a needle I would like to deposit with you. Please guard it, and you can give it back to me in the other world."

The banker, surprised by this curious request, laughed. "You are so ignorant. Nobody has ever been able to take anything to the other world."

"Who is ignorant, you or me? You spend all your time accumulating wealth that you can't take with you. Whereas I am looking for what I can take with me," Nanak replied lovingly.

"Please," begged the rich man, "accept my invitation. Teach me the true path of life and show me the way that will lead me to peace. Despite all my possessions I remain unsatisfied."

This time Nanak agreed to follow him, and they continued the conversation.

Having understood Nanak's divine words, the banker gave himself up and fell at Nanak's feet. With tears in his eyes he said, "O great master, save me. Remove the mud of material wealth in which I am mired. Pull me out of this dreadful swamp and grant me the favour of the eternal word."

His faith and his love of truth were rewarded. He received the communion he wanted so much. Nanak said to him before leaving, "Remember that what you give is yours, and what you keep is not yours."

38. RETURN TO PUNJAB AND REUNION

After re-entering the desert of Rajasthan, Nanak, Bala and Mardana marched to the north towards the Punjab region they had left so many years earlier. The journey back from village to village was uneventful and peaceful. At each stage, Nanak sowed the seed of eternal Name in the hearts of the people, kings, and those who aspired to appease their souls. And so, after twelve years of absence, Nanak and his companions finally reached their village, Talvandi, in the year 1512.

You will never believe what Nanak announced. "I will not enter the village; I'll stay here."

Mardana, totally confused, begged and implored him, "Me, I'd like to see my family and my friends. Can you allow me to go there?"

"Of course. It is I who broke ties with my family and material things. Don't tell my family," Nanak advised him.

Mardana was overjoyed to see his wife, his children and his friends. The news spread like wildfire, and everyone came running. They touched Mardana's feet out of respect and asked him where Nanak was. Then Mardana went to see Tripta, Nanak's mother.

"Where is my son? Tell me about Nanak," pleaded Tripta.

But Mardana continued to talk about other things and carefully avoided the subject. He quickly returned to Nanak. Tripta guessed that her son was not far away. She took some food and discreetly followed Mardana. Outside the village she found Nanak sitting on the ground. When he saw his mother, he touched her feet, got up, and kissed her tenderly. Tripta's eyes flooded with tears of joy. She hugged Nanak for a long time.

"I am proud of you, son. I'm glad to see your face," said the mother. "All these years, I thought of you. I was worried that my only son had left his home and become an ascetic."

A crowd of people followed Tripta. Many came from far away to see Nanak and hear his words. All rejoiced at the end of this long separation.

Tripta offered the food she had brought to Nanak. "Eat what I have prepared with much love."

Nanak replied, "Mother, I thank you, but I am full forever, filled with the love of Name. I'm never hungry."

The news also reached the ears of his father Kalu, who hastened to see his son. Kalu had not yet understood his son's mission and hoped that he would put an end to his wanderings and take life a little more seriously.

Nanak touched his father's feet and then embraced him.

"Son, come home. We have rebuilt the house. Come see. Put away your fakir's clothes and put on some decent clothes."

Nanak sang:

The Name is my red clothes;
Virtue and charity are my white clothes;

124

My blue tunic allows me to cleanse the spiritual dirt
And to meditate at God's feet;
Contentment is my belt, and God's Name is my wealth and my youth.

"Don't be unreasonable," Kalu said. "You have travelled enough. I'm going to buy a good horse for you, and you should take charge of the business and start to manage it."

Tripta added lovingly, "My son, I know you have no attachment to worldly things. But still, come to the house we have built for you. After you have lived with us a little, you will regain the love of your family and become happy."

In response Nanak sang:

The bliss of Name is my house;
The grace of God is my family.

"Dear mother, my mind is still discontented. I would like to travel more and visit other countries before settling down here for good."

Nervous, Kalu spoke, "We are old now and unable to continue working. Our end is near. If you leave again, we will never see you."

"Listen, my son," said Tripta, "don't be stubborn. Come home; my eyes are never satiated seeing you. If you don't like it, you can leave again."

These words of love overruled Nanak's resolve, and he went home. A few days later his wife and his two sons and his sister Nanki were overjoyed to see him again. All the villagers came to seek Nanak's blessing. All celebrated the reunion to their hearts' content.

One day, Kalu reminded Nanak, "I'm old now. I can't work. You must leave your ascetic lifestyle and take up your family responsibility." But despite this reminder, Kalu met only with his son's determination to pursue his divine mission.

Actually, it was during Nanak's brief stay in Talvandi that his father understood his son's thoughts. By Nanak's grace the mist of Kalu's illusion dissipated. His parents marvelled and saw divine light shining in all things.

Not long afterwards both Kalu and Tripta died.

One day, Nanak's friend Rai Bular, the village chief, wanted to see him. The chief was also quite old and felt the end was near. When he saw Nanak, he tried to get up from his bed, but his strength failed him. With tear-filled eyes he murmured, "In spirit, I am at your feet, but the flesh is weak."

Nanak was deeply touched by this love. Full of compassion, Nanak put his hand on the chief's head. Rai Bular's soul left his body, rising to heaven beyond the cycle of death and birth.

Thus, after staying among his family and his friends, Nanak resumed his journey and his work, always accompanied by his faithful companions Bala and Mardana.

39. THE PUNDIT WHO KNEW TOO MUCH

Over the years, Nanak attracted many disciples. He realized that they needed a place to live. That is when Nanak founded Kartarpur, the city of the Creator, in order to welcome and lodge them. Then in 1513 he began his second journey. Nanak was forty-four years old. This time he went to the North, accompanied by his two loyal friends, Bala and Mardana. First, they visited the towns and villages of Punjab and then headed for Tibet. Everywhere he went, Nanak spoke to people in the same way, whether they were Hindus, Muslims or Buddhists. People gathered to listen to his words of love and faith and willingly accepted his teachings.

After several days' march they reached the beautiful valley of Lahaul and Spiti in the Himalayas. From here they could travel over the

Parang pass to Ladakh and Tibet. Along the way they visited the villages of Malana, Chaumurti and Boling. Everywhere people gathered around Nanak, fascinated by his appearance and by his words.

Nanak's aim was to go to Kailash, the sacred Hindu mountain. Nearby there were many sects of ascetics and yogis. Each sect and each yogi specialized in some religious subject. Some were proud of their knowledge, others claimed that he could reach any place anywhere in the blink of eye. Others could perform miracles, even fly like birds. They were rather magicians than holy men. They were convinced that they were on the true godly path, and they did not want anyone to meddle in their activities. Nanak had already heard of these men, and this was why he wanted to meet them.

First, he encountered a pundit, Brahm Das. This pundit was so proud that he did not want people like Nanak even to go near him. He always travelled with numerous books on Indian wisdom, loaded on three camels. He considered himself to be a great scholar, always thirsty to read more. He acted as though it was a waste of time and useless to meet with a stranger just passing by. One day Brahm Das went to a nearby forest to visit his friend Kamal, a Muslim fakir. Kamal told him about a strange visitor he had met a little earlier. Kamal was a very godly man always looking for the truth. After conversations with Nanak his veil of illusion disappeared, and he saw the light and felt immense joy. He realized that he had been wasting his time and effort in the forest.

Brahm Das was so intrigued by the change in his friend that he decided to talk to Nanak. He approached him with his books, hoping to have a real discussion about his scholarship. He found Nanak singing to the strains of Mardana's rebab:

Even reading all the books on the carts of a caravan;
Even studying the books on a whole fleet of boats;
Even filling all the caves of the Earth with volumes of books;
Even reading month after month, year after year, a lifetime;
All this is vain and remains vanity as long as God is not recognized.

The pundit was deeply moved by these words because they reflected his own state and his pride.

Brahm Das could not hold back his tears and fell at Nanak's feet. "Forgive me," he said, "I have read and reread sacred books and acquired academic knowledge of the six schools of philosophy, but I confess that I have not found inner peace. I beg you, O master, bless me, show me the light and give me peace, as you have done for Kamal."

Nanak lovingly gave him the heavenly vision, and Brahm Das became one of the staunchest preachers of the holy word in the Kashmir valley.

40. SADHUS WHO COULD FLY

On the way to Tibet, Nanak and his friends came to a Buddhist monastery. The senior Lama welcomed them warmly. For many hours they discussed spiritual matters evoking thoughts of the Buddha. The Lama asked Nanak, "You claim that the absolute God is infinite. Then how can a limited creature merge with the unlimited?"

"In the same way that the tree and its fruit are similar," replied Nanak. "Those who taste the fruit hanging on the tree of immortality and drink its nectar are one with God. One who identifies with the individual soul is one with the supreme soul."

"I like what you say," said the Lama. "Your words are like rays of light piercing the darkness of the mind."

After taking leave of the Lama, our friends continued their journey towards Mount Kailash and reached the valley of Sumer, the land of eternal snow. In that place, they encountered many sadhus and yogis who had settled there to escape the corrupt political climate prevailing in the plains of India at that time. Curious, Nanak inquired, "If you hide yourself in the solitude of the mountains, who will teach the people the right path to follow?"

After long discussions with the sadhus and pilgrims on the shores of Lake Mansarovar, Nanak talked with hermits living in mountain caves. On reaching Almora they camped near a small cluster of cottages of a yogi clan. Its chief was named Gorakh Nath. Nearly everyone in this clan was a corrupt magician. One of them, Bharthari, had met Nanak before. He informed Gorakh of Nanak's arrival and said, "Nanak is a truly holy man. You must convince him to join our group and become your disciple. If you succeed, you will become the most powerful yogi."

Gorakh decided to go himself to meet Nanak and convert him. He asked Nanak, "Who are you? What's your caste? Why have you come here? Where will you go? Listen to me, turn around and go back immediately before death devours you. You'll not see the sun here. There are ogres who will swallow you whole."

Nanak replied calmly, "We are curious explorers and have no caste. Our country is where neither the moon nor the sun shines. We travel wherever it pleases us. We are not afraid of anything anymore. In our eyes, misfortune and happiness are the same. God, the sole creator, is our guru. Gorakh, you seem to be quite lost. At your old age you should not be so arrogant."

Gorakh was livid with anger, but he tried not to show it. He replied as calmly as possible, "Come, join my clan of yogis. You will become immortal and you will acquire extraordinary powers. All your desires will be satisfied. You will rule over everything."

"I have already abandoned the 'I' in me. I no longer need my body. Magical powers are inferior to the Name. And we have no desire to be adored by crowds."

Deeply offended, Gorakh tried to use his magic to topple the stone on which Nanak was sitting. Despite several attempts, the stone did not budge one inch. The great yogi understood then that Nanak was an extraordinary person. Gorakh suddenly disappeared, as if dissolved in the air casting a total darkness over the three.

Amazed, Mardana spoke, "Master, there is no sun or moon! Where are we?"

Without saying a word Nanak began to walk toward Gorakh's cottage. Gorakh had gathered all his disciples in front of him. One of them was sitting on a deer skin, another on a lion's skin, a third wore a necklace of bones, and another was completely coated with ash. One man standing at the back wore large glass earrings. Then there was one who could turn himself into a fierce animal or an ogre. The last disciple had the ability to fly. In short, each of them possessed a special magic power.

Gorakh spoke, "Nanak is coming to meet us. Is there someone among you who can hold him and convince him to become my disciple? Because if he joins my clan, I'd be even more respected everywhere."

The yogis who boasted of their magical powers were Machinder, Bhander, Hanifa, Charpat, Jhangar, Sanghar, Sambhalka, Gopi Chand, Ishar Nath, Langar, Mangal and Shanbhu. Together, they devised a plan to approach Nanak and seduce him. One by one, they went to meet

Nanak. Each one used his arguments and magical powers to convince him. But none of them managed to side track Nanak, not even a little.

Against all odds, the yogi named Mangal listened to Nanak's wise teachings and became his disciple.

Finally, Gorakh decided to send Bharthari to Nanak. "All the sadhus wish to see you. They are waiting for you," said Bharthari.

"Well, tell them that I am on my way," said Nanak. Soon Nanak entered the assembly and greeted Gorakh, "I salute you."

"Greetings to you too," replied Gorakh, who very respectfully invited our friends to sit with him. He asked Bharthari to bring a drink containing some drug. He wanted to intoxicate Nanak.

Nanak asked, "What kind of drink is this?"

Gorakh replied, "It is nectar. When you drink it, you'll fall into a deep trance. The fear of death will disappear. You will never feel hunger or thirst. You'll pass into the fourth sphere, which will allow you to use all the magical powers that exist. Then you will hear the heavenly music and you'll become immortal."

"How do you make this nectar?" asked Nanak.

A sadhu named Jhangar explained the process of distillation and added, "If you drink this nectar, misfortune and grief will turn into perpetual happiness."

Nanak said, "Your nectar does not attract me. Those who drink it are not wise. For me, my nectar is the fruit of understanding, heated by twigs that are the good deeds in the oven of knowledge. The nectar is drawn with love focused on awareness, and it fills the pot of compassion. He who drinks this goblet of peace becomes connected with God."

The debate lasted several days. The yogis wanted Nanak to join them and adopt their cult. But the master explained to them by singing:

The true yogi is not recognized by the clothes he wears,
Or the stick on which he leans to walk,
Or the way he covers his body with ashes;
Yoga is not wearing earrings,
Shaving your head, or blowing into a conch;
The true yogi does not withdraw to caves or glaciers;
He does not sit on mats practicing various postures,

Nor wander from place to place,
Nor seek to purify himself in sacred rivers;
Living in the everyday world, pure and free from any vice,
You will then walk on the trail of the truth.

A small group of yogis fell under the spell of Nanak's singing and his words. He explained that the thirst of desires cannot be quenched by leaving family life and daily problems. The family is the real school of life. We engage consciously in the duties of a house holder.

Five other yogis submitted to Nanak's teachings, and they felt an extraordinary joy. But others who were more arrogant resisted and tried to impress everyone with their magic tricks. One sent his deer skin mat into the air; another launched the wooden seat he used during meditation; others sent into the air their horns, earrings and beggar's bowls. All these strange objects whirled in the sky at the speed of sound, making squealing noises. Mardana plugged his ears with his fingers and turned pale with fear. Nanak observed the scene without saying a word. Yogis interpreted his silence as a sign of defeat and submission. They were sure that Nanak and his two friends would run away. The most arrogant yogi spoke to Nanak, "Our power has silenced you. Give up your unnecessary words. Wear the earrings, cover your body with ash, and accept Gorakh as your guru. Otherwise we will kill you with our power. You can choose now."

Do you think that Nanak was frightened? Not in the least.

Nanak spoke to his left shoe, "Rise up into the sky and send all the objects back to their owners."

The shoe flew up instantly, and every flying object fell in front of the yogi to whom it belonged. Then Nanak's shoe returned to his foot. Stunned, the yogis all sat there with their mouths agape.

From that moment, Gorakh accepted the fact that Nanak was a truly saintly person. The two of them discussed spiritual issues for several days.

It is said that the branches of the bitter cherry tree that provided Nanak with shade during his stay at this place produced extraordinarily sweet cherries, while the cherries on the rest of the tree kept their natural bitter taste.

Our friends took their leave of Gorakh. Several yogis would have liked to have Nanak stay and live with them. But Nanak had other regions to visit.

Endnote: Yogis reject family life and escape from society. They are afraid of assuming normal social responsibilities. Nanak was not a yogi. He wanted to put such people on the right path. He missed his family very much during his long travels. At the end of his journey he returned to live with his family (see Story 46).

41. FAKIR VALI KANDAHARI'S FRESHWATER SPRING

Nanak and his two friends walked fifty kilometres around Mount Kailash and then turned to the northwest towards the source of the River Indus. They descended along the valley, passed through the village of Gyantse, and then made a little foray into the Chinese land. Returning to the valley, they stopped in several populated places. One such place was Basgo, where, according to local tradition, Nanak was attacked by a giant. Surprised, Nanak pushed the giant against a rock wall; the imprint the giant left in the rock still exists. They left the Himalayas through Kargil and passed through the village of Kankhal. A path brought them to Srinagar, the capital of Kashmir on Dal Lake, universally known for its beauty. In Punjab they stopped in Hassan Abdal, a major city near Rawalpindi. It was a very hot day and an unusual event was about to take place.

"Master, I am thirsty," complained Mardana. "I can't walk."

"We'll rest at the foot of the hill you see in front of us," said Nanak calmly. "On the top of this hill lives a fakir, a very pious person. He is known in the region for his supernatural power, of which he is very proud. He rarely leaves his hut. The city people come to listen to him. A freshwater spring flows in his garden, and he has built a small reservoir for his needs."

The fakir's name was Vali Kandahari, a Sufi of the Shiite sect. He despised Sunnis and people of other beliefs. In particular, he did not at all like it that another holy man had come to the region to preach.

"Mardana, we'll first sing and thank God for having brought us back safely to our country. Pick up your rebab," said Nanak.

Listening to the melodious song, a number of inhabitants of the city were drawn to Nanak. Vali Kandahari, who saw everything from the hill, went into a wild rage.

Mardana complained again that he was very thirsty. Nanak said to him, "Go up that hill and ask the person at the top to give you water."

At the top Mardana heard a voice, "Who are you?"

"My name is Mardana and I am a disciple of Nanak. He is sitting at the bottom of this hill. I am thirsty, so he told me to come see you."

Vali Kandahari was upset to learn that a holy man was in his region and that he did not even come up and pay him homage.

"There is no water for people like you," the fakir shouted. "Go back to your master. If he really is a holy man, he should give you water."

Poor Mardana reported to Nanak what had happened.

"Don't worry. Go up once again and this time ask him humbly for some water." Mardana, tired and thirsty, did not dare to disobey. He clambered to the top of the hill. Vexed, the fakir again sent him back, warning him of all the misfortunes that could befall him if he continued to stay with an infidel.

Nanak smiled as the downcast Mardana approached. He advised him not to lose courage and patience.

That said, Nanak dug a hole in the ground and looked towards the top of the hill. O miracle! A jet of crystal-clear water suddenly sprang from the ground. At the same time, the fakir noticed that his reservoir's water level was rapidly sinking, until there was not a single drop left. Confused, the fakir looked down the hill, where he saw water gushing from an unknown spring. The fakir became furious.

Using his supernatural power, he pushed a huge rock that rolled in the direction of Nanak. Undaunted, Nanak sat quietly. When the stone was about to crush him, he simply reached out with his hand, and the rock stopped at the touch of his palm.

Seeing this miracle, Vali Kandahari was awestruck. He ran down the hill with long strides and begged Nanak's forgiveness.

"My friend," said Nanak. "Those who seek to live in high places should not be hard as rock."

A long discussion ensued, and the fakir became an enthusiastic follower of Name. He stopped despising people of other beliefs. The print of Nanak's palm—panja—on the stone is still visible, and water continues to flow where he dug the hole. A Gurdwara, a Sikh temple, was built at this place, now known as Panja Sahib in present-day Pakistan.

42. THE DEBATE WITH THE SAGE MIAN MITDU

From Hassan Abdal city, Nanak, Bala and Mardana branched off southward in the direction of their village of Talvandi, still a long walk of several weeks. Before crossing the River Jhelum, they paused at Bal Gudai, an important centre of sidhas, Hindu yogis, with whom Nanak had long debates focused, as always, on spirituality. Nanak summed up these debates in a long poem, *Sidh Gost* (dialogue with sidhas), which can be read in the *Adi Granth*, the Sikh holy book. Some people believe that even today the marks left by Nanak's feet can still be seen at the place where he sat.

The trio took the Royal Shah Rah road to cross the rivers Jhelum and Chenab and arrived in Sialkot, then the capital of Punjab. Once settled in, Nanak gave Mardana two silver coins and told him, "Go into town and buy the truth with one coin and a lie with the other."

Poor Mardana had never heard of such a thing. Anyway, off he went. Mardana stopped in several shops and asked, "Do you have the truth or a lie to sell?"

"Are you sick? They do not exist," the shopkeepers mocked.

But Mardana did not give up. He entered the shop of a man named Moolla. He took the two silver coins inside and came out with two small sheets of paper. On the first was written "death is the truth" and on the other "life is a lie."

Mardana brought his purchase to Nanak, who was very impressed. Immediately, he went to see Moolla.

"You really understand the meaning of life. I congratulate you," said Nanak.

"I still have a lot to learn," answered Moolla. "And with your help, I can learn more." Moolla was so moved by Nanak's words that he closed his shop and left with him.

A few days of walking brought them to Kotla, where they met a Muslim sage, Mian Mitdu, a scholar of Islamic tradition who was very knowledgeable about divine issues. When Mian Mitdu heard that his friend Nanak was coming, he hastened to meet him. He found Nanak sitting comfortably in a pretty garden. Very quickly they renewed their friendship. They talked at length about the role of the Koran and the prophet Mohammed.

"The Almighty Allah is the highest, then comes the prophet," argued Mian Mitdu. "If you recite the Koran, you'll be accepted in Allah's court."

Nanak replied, "The highest is the Name of Allah. The prophet serves at its door."

Mian Mitdu remarked, "One cannot light a lamp without oil. In the same way, without the prophet one cannot find salvation and be accepted by Allah."

Nanak recited his poem:

How can the lamp cast light without oil?
The practice of the wisdom of the sacred books is the oil;
Insert the wick of the fear of God in this body, lamp,
And light the lamp of life using the torch of understanding of the
eternal truth.

Mian Mitda was so touched that he became a disciple and friend of Nanak.

43. THE MASSACRE OF SAIDPUR AND THE MIRACLE OF THE BUNDLE

Continuing their journey on Pasrur road, Nanak and his companions reached Saidpur once again. This city, now in Pakistan, is called Eminabad. Do you remember that Nanak had stayed here with Lalo the Carpenter, who lived a little way outside this city? This time, too, they stayed with him. The city was inhabited largely by the Pathans, an ethnic group that ruled the country. They led a luxurious life, not caring much for poor people. Nanak knew what was going to happen to this city, and he warned its inhabitants.

"I am coming from the North, where I learned that a Mughal warlord, Emir Zahir ud-din Muhammad, known as Babur, is preparing to invade us. He is the descendant of Timor the Terrible. After he lost his kingdom in Turkmenistan, he conquered Khorasan and Kabul. But that was not enough for him. He now wants to conquer Punjab and the whole of India. The city of Sialkot has already sent a message of submission in order to escape being ravaged and plundered. But Babur is attracted by prosperous Saidpur. We must all get out of here."

Several people followed his advice and left the city. They were lucky, because soon after, out of nowhere,

Babur's army forced its way into Saidpur. It was the year 1521. There was great panic everywhere. The Mughal attackers were extremely violent. They massacred people and looted everything they could lay their hands. They killed Muslims and Hindu men; they captured women and children and made them work as slaves. Babur forced them to carry the plundered goods to his home in Afghanistan.

Nanak and Mardana were also imprisoned. Luckily, a few days earlier, Bala and Moolla had taken leave to return to their village. We do not know where Bala was at that time. Mardana was ordered to take care of commander Mir Khan's horse. He walked behind Nanak, who was carrying a heavy bundle on his head.

"Take out your rebab and play," said Nanak to Mardana.

"Master, I can't, I am holding the horse."

"Drop the reins," said Nanak, who started to sing.

Mir Khan, who was watching, was stunned to see that his horse was quietly following Mardana and that Nanak's bundle floated in the air, about thirty centimetres above his head.

Nanak was deeply distressed by the blind rage of one people against another. He wept bitterly, because he wanted the massacre to stop and he wanted to share the pain of the suffering people taken prisoner along with hundreds of other people. Nanak was led to a camp where men and women were forced to turn hand mills to grind wheat into flour all day long in order to feed the soldiers. This hard work continued amid cries of pain and wailing of the wounded. Later, Nanak voiced his complaint to God in a poem:

When the invaders inflicted such suffering,
And people cried out in piercing screams,
Did you not, O God, feel compassion?

Nanak himself was filled with the deepest compassion towards his unfortunate fellow prisoners. He tried with all his heart to soothe their pain with sweet words, providing them with hope. Listening to him, prisoners forgot their misery. To better hear Nanak, little by little they stopped turning their mills. But by some miracle the mills continued to turn by themselves. When he witnessed this, Mir Khan immediately informed Babur, and the invader hastened to see the strange scene himself. He noticed that all of his men, including the guards, were under the sway of the gentle charm of Nanak's song. For all his belligerence and brutality, Babur felt powerless in the face of Nanak's sweetness and love. At the sight of the miraculous mills he swallowed his pride and humbly spoke to Nanak, "Holy man, you are a true representative of God. I will do anything you want."

"I am hungry for God," replied Nanak. "I do not need anything. Instead, free these poor people whom you have cruelly oppressed and ruined."

Babur felt deep remorse. A new and sincere conscience awoke in him. He immediately released all prisoners and tried to redeem himself as much as he could by distributing the fortune he had amassed.

Babur then invited Nanak to his tent and offered him a glass of wine.

"My cup is full to the brim," Nanak replied. "I am satisfied with the wine of divine love and in this way, I stay intoxicated day and night."

44. MECCA MOVES

Nanak had travelled for more than twenty years and had visited the whole of India up to Assam, Burma in the east and Sri Lanka in the south. In the north he had walked across the Himalayas to visit Tibet and China. Our trio of friends were tireless.

And the west? For a short while they stayed with their families. But a new adventure awaited them. Moolla, who had sold the truth and the lie to Mardana and abandoned his family to follow Nanak, decided to return to Sialkot.

One day, Mardana spoke to Nanak: "Master I am old. My end is not far off. With you I have seen the world. I have one desire that I would like to fulfil, just one."

"Tell me, Mardana."

"Every Muslim's wish is to make a pilgrimage to Mecca before leaving this earthly life."

Nanak needed no better excuse to travel to the west, to Muslim countries.

During his travels, Nanak dressed like a roving religious man, a fakir. Bhai Gurdas, a scholar-poet of the same era, stated that for his trip to Mecca "Nanak dressed in the blue clothes of a Muslim pilgrim Haji. In one hand he held an earthen cup for his ablutions, and under his arm, the holy book and his prayer rug." This way of dressing was necessary because it was forbidden for non-Muslims to enter the Kaaba, the most sacred Muslim place, in Mecca. However, in the 16th century, even non-Muslims were allowed to visit Mecca.

The families of Nanak, Mardana and Bala were saddened once again. But for Nanak it was a call from God, and they headed west. Nanak went to Sultanpur to see his sister Nanki. There, he met the Chief Daulat Khan, his former employer and close friend. Then they followed the River Sutlej to the city of Multan. It was the second time they were taking this road. In Pakpatan Nanak was delighted to see his friend Pir Ibrahim. They embraced warmly. For several days they discussed spiritual ideas.

Ibrahim referred to the works of his grandfather, Sheikh Farid, who had composed 112 divine verses of great beauty in the Punjabi language. They were the first known composition written in this language. Farid addressed these verses to himself, so as not to criticize others. Ibrahim recited some of them.

Nanak was so touched by Farid's words that he asked if he could have the manuscript. With great pleasure and without hesitation Ibrahim offered him the gift. These verses have been incorporated in the *Adi Granth*, the holy book of the Sikhs.

Nanak followed the Hajj route and arrived at the sacred Muslim city of Multan. There he met Sheikh Makhdum Baha-ud-din, and they discussed many things. The Sheikh acknowledged that Nanak considered Hindus and Muslims equal before God. Nanak bade farewell to the Makhdum and went to Uch, the third sacred center of Muslim Sufis. Sheikh Haji Abdul Bukhari greeted them with much love. A few days later Baha-ud-din joined them, and they all took the Hajj route. They followed the Indus River and reached the port of Lakhpat at its mouth on the Arabian Sea. A small coastal boat took them to Miani eighty kilometres north of Karachi. There they were joined by several other Indian Muslim hajjis. A big Arab dhow carried them across the Gulf of Oman and skirted the coast of the Arabian Peninsula to the city of Aden and the Red Sea.

Nanak, always accompanied by his two friends, stopped in Jeddah, the port nearest to Mecca. The long trek in the hot desert country was exhausting. Finally, they reached their destination—Mecca, site of the sacred black stone of Kaaba. According to Muslim tradition this is the abode of Allah himself.

One day in this sacred city, Nanak suddenly felt tired and lay down on the ground with his feet turned in the direction of the Kaaba. This action is considered by Muslims to be extremely sacrilegious. If caught, an offender could be put to death.

Do you really think that Nanak did not know what he was doing? As always, he had done this on purpose.

One of the Sufis accompanying him woke Nanak and asked him to quickly change the direction of his feet before the grand Qadi found out. But someone had already informed the Qadi, who was furious. Followed by armed men, he stormed to the sacred site and rebuked Nanak, "You're an infidel! Why have you pointed your feet in the direction of the house of God?"

Now wide awake, Nanak replied, "For me, the whole world is the house of God. Now if you want, turn my feet in the direction where there is no God!"

Extremely angry, Qadi Rukun-ud-din himself firmly grabbed Nanak's feet and turned them in a different direction, away from the

Kaaba. But when he lifted his head, he could not believe his eyes. To his amazement, he saw the Kaaba in the direction of the feet that he had just turned. And everywhere he pointed them he saw the house of God.

Did the Kaaba really move? Or had Nanak influenced the minds of the people so that they saw things differently?

Rukun-ud-din proclaimed, "How wonderful! Today I have in truth met the man of God."

Then the Makhdum of Pakpatan, who had accompanied Nanak to Mecca, bowed to him and prayed. "I would love to keep your sandals as a memento."

Nanak offered them willingly. His sandals were then carefully taken to India. You can see them at the Dargah (Muslim monastery) of Uch in present-day Pakistan.

Nanak said, "See, the house of God is in all directions. He remains in every place and in every heart. He is not imprisoned in a mosque or a temple."

The next day, Nanak was surrounded by many curious people who came to listen to the one who had performed the miracle of Kaaba. One of them asked Nanak, "I see that you are from India. What is your religion?"

Nanak replied, "I am no more Hindu than Muslim. I belong to that which is Unique, who is the master of creation and who permeates all things, one who has not experienced birth and who will not experience death."

Endnote: Nanak did not accept the existence of a unique sacred space. For him every place was sacred.

45. MARDANA LAUGHS AT DEATH

From Mecca our pilgrims headed for Medina, where the prophet Mohammed is buried. Mardana went to visit his tomb and he took Nanak with him.

After resting a few days, the trio decided not to take the popular caravan route to Baghdad via Damascus. Instead, they followed the more difficult but shorter road taken by hajis, pilgrims. In those days, Persians governed Baghdad, and the Sunnis and Shiites fought violently. Nanak, who spoke fluent Farsi, decided to settle on the west bank of the Euphrates River. The main town was on the opposite bank.

In this city, Nanak had long and fruitful discussions with Bahlol, a Muslim holy man who became an ardent follower of Nanak. It is said that Bahlol spent sixty years of his life in the place where Nanak had rested.

A small altar erected to the memory of Nanak can be visited today on the outskirts of Baghdad. Later, other evidence of Nanak's passage was discovered. It is said that King Murad created a plaque to commemorate Nanak's visit to this place. This is the inscription:

When he saw that the monument dedicated to the memory of Hazrat Rab-i-majid, Baba Nanak, Aulya-i-Allah (the Prophet of God) lay in ruins, Murad, by the grace of God all powerful, rebuilt the monument with his own hands so that this fountain of well-being could continue to refresh the generations to come.

Having delighted the people and saints of many oases, the fakirs of rose gardens, and the people of Arabia, Iraq and Persia, Nanak, Bala and Mardana finally turned toward India. On the way they visited the ancient city of Tabriz, then Tehran and Mashhad. In Mashhad the Shiite religious leader Pir Abdul Rehman said to Nanak, "You are in the land of the Shiites. Are you a Shiite or a Sunni?"

Nanak replied, "The divine light shines within us all. For me, all the prophets are equal. But we do not see it, because we are blinded by wickedness and passion."

When they had left the city of Mashhad, Mardana said, "Master, we have travelled a lot. Now we should hurry back home."

"You are thinking of your home, Mardana. If you want, we can get you there instantly," replied Nanak.

"No, I'd like to go with you; I don't want to go back alone."

Joking with Mardana, Nanak said, "In any case, you're going to get there first and thus escape from the comings and goings of this world."

Mardana understood what he meant. "Tell me, where will my body rest? How long am I to live?" asked Mardana, laughing.

"Only five days are left."

"Will you be there with me?"

"Of course I'll be with you."

Four days later our travellers arrived in Afghanistan. That night Mardana dreamed that Muslims who were buried there were burned when they arrived in the afterlife. In the morning he said to Nanak, "To spare me from being burned later, burn my body here on earth."

"I'd do anything you desire," promised Nanak. "You still have some time. Your destiny is for you first to enjoy a good dinner in the town of Kuram, which you see in front of us. You are going to leave your body in this place."

At Kuram, Nanak said to Mardana, "Enjoy your last meal."

When Mardana had finished eating, they went to a beautiful and quiet place and sat on a platform. Nanak spoke, "How are you feeling?"

"I'm ready," Mardana replied and knelt before Nanak.

Nanak then asked, "How do you know that your time has come, Mardana?"

"By accompanying you I have learned to understand my body. My breath is getting short. I am starting to breathe my last breaths. Now only nine are left. You can count if you want."

Nanak asked Bala to count. At the end of the ninth breath only Mardana's body remained, at peace. Such a gentle death happens only

149

with a saintly person. With much love and affection, Nanak and Bala wrapped Mardana's body in a white cloth, placed it on a pile of dry wood and cremated it.

As you know, Mardana was a superb rebab player and a remarkable singer. Even now he is always lovingly referred to as "Bhai"—brother—Mardana.

Endnote: Actually, Mardana died in 1534, many years after his travels, in Talvandi (India) and not in Kuram (Afghanistan).

46. RETURN TO FAMILY LIFE

Without Mardana's company and his voice, Nanak and Bala's journey was much less enjoyable and interesting. They took the old caravan road and came to the city of Balkh, near Mazari-sharif, and then headed south to Kabul. Leaving Afghanistan, they crossed the Kurram Pass and reached Peshawar in India. The famous Khyber Pass was not opened until several years later. When they arrived at Lahore, instead of heading to his village, Talvandi, Nanak walked in the exact opposite direction to get to a magnificent place on the River Ravi, eighty kilometres from Lahore. I hope you remember that he had named this place Kartarpur, the Creator's place, a village he had founded before starting his last journey.

It is here that Nanak spent the last part of his life. He put away his traveller's clothes and put on those of a Punjabi villager. Until his last breath he cultivated the land. His wife Sulakhani and his two adult sons, Sri Chand and Lakhmi Das, joined him. He wanted to show by his example that human beings can associate his spiritual quest with his daily work. He used to say, "Only those who earn their living honestly can know God."

Many people began to gather around him and work the land nearby. At dawn all would gather to listen to Nanak's teachings. He introduced the concept of "langar" the community kitchen. Rich and poor, Hindus and Muslims, Brahmins and untouchables—all sat together, without distinction, and enjoyed the same food.

More people started coming from the four corners of the country to listen to him. Contemplation of Name, love and work, silence, and singing became a rhythm of life in Kartarpur.

One day a man by the name of Lehna passed by Kartarpur on his way to Jawalaji to worship the goddess Durga. He heard Nanak singing and was so charmed that he abandoned his pilgrimage and became his disciple. Nanak soon discovered that Lehna was a good person, intelligent, full of faith, and ready to serve the community at any time.

Nanak found that Lehna achieved more than Nanak's own two sons in all the activities and tests he imposed. Soon Lehna learned the writing style of his guru and began to compose devotional songs.

Nanak took Lehna with him to see Moolla in Sialkot. When they stopped in front of the house, Moolla's wife saw them and became frightened. She ran to warn her husband, "The fakirs you went away with once are in front of the house. I don't want you to leave me again. Go hide in the back of the house before they see you!"

Moolla rushed off and hid in a pile of dried cow dung.

Nanak called aloud, "Moolla, oh Moolla, are you there?"

The woman replied, "No, he's gone shopping in the city."

"What a shame, I wanted to meet him, but he preferred to listen to his wife and hide and avoid talking to me." Then he added, "Death comes without warning. I'm afraid I will not see him again." After a little reflection they left.

There are two stories of what happened to Moolla.

Some say that a cobra that was sheltering in the freshness of the stack of dried dung bit Moolla. He screamed in pain and accused his wife, "It is you who prevented me from seeing Nanak. Now I'm going to die because of your lies. Take me to Nanak so that I can apologize."

Then he fell on the ground and fainted. Neighbours quickly carried him to the place where Nanak was sitting. Moolla's wife begged, "Forgive us and save my husband!"

In the other version of this story, Moolla had recognized Nanak's voice. Feeling very guilty, he asked his wife if Nanak had left. His wife replied, "Yes, it's good, isn't it?" Moolla was so chagrined that he collapsed. Some people gathered around him, and one of them found that he was dead.

"We must tell Nanak!" he said.

Soon afterward Nanak appeared. Moolla's wife pleaded with Nanak to revive her husband. Nanak said, "His time on earth has ended. One can do nothing against God's will."

47. THE END OF THE JOURNEY

Finally, it was Nanak's turn. The day he would die was not far off. He managed his own farm and encouraged others to engage in honest work. People of all faiths, rich and poor, came to see him and listen to him. Nanak's two sons, well-bred and educated, participated in all the community activities.

But they were pretentious. Unlike Lehna, they showed no humility. As we have already learned, Nanak tested all three many times. Each time it was Lehna who was the best. Nanak's wife Sulakhani noticed that Nanak was favouring Lehna and preparing him for his succession. One day she asked him why, and Nanak replied, "Spiritual and community views are not hereditary. It is the quality of a person that counts."

At that moment a cat passed by close to the gathering. It was carrying a half-devoured rat in its mouth. People cried out loudly, and the frightened cat dropped its prey and fled. Nanak said to his son Sri Chand, "Go and get rid of that rat!"

"I have no desire to touch a dead rat!" replied Sri Chand. Then Nanak asked Lakhmi Das to do the same.

"How can I touch a dead rat? I can ask someone else to do it."

Nanak turned to Lehna. Before Nanak said a word, Lehna rushed over and threw the rat outside.

Nanak said to his wife, "Lehna is blessed by God, and he is the only one who can continue my mission."

A few days later Nanak took Lehna to the River Ravi. Nanak waded into the water and remained standing, while Lehna stayed on the bank sitting cross-legged in meditation. At that moment the two spirits entered into a communion. This is how Lehna became part of Nanak and was named "Angad," a part of his body.

The news spread fast, and a huge crowd gathered to hear for the last time the sweet words of the one who had changed the fate of so many people. Nanak was sitting, serene and beaming, in front of the gathering. He explained that his mission had been completed, and he invited everyone to rejoice with him to the end of his earthly journey and his return to the eternal home. A feeling of peace came over the crowd and a divine music arose to accompany Nanak to the celestial spheres. When the haze of this sublime moment dissipated, some people began to quarrel. The Muslims wanted to bury the remains of the guru, while the Hindus were asking for his cremation. Before lying down and covering himself with a sheet, Nanak told them, "Each group should place a vase of flowers next to my body. If tomorrow morning the flowers of the Hindus fade, the Muslims will take my body, and if those of the Muslims fade, then the Hindus will take it." Then Nanak pulled the sheet over himself.

The next day the instigators of this dispute felt deeply ashamed when someone lifted the white sheet. Everyone was amazed to see that the body of Nanak had disappeared and that all the flowers remained fresh as before. In a final act, Nanak had reminded the crowd of his message.

In the year 1539 he left his earthly body-shell after a stay of seventy years.

The white sheet was cut and shared between Hindus and Muslims. According to their respective traditions, two tombs were built next to each other. Later a severe flood of the River Ravi effaced these memorials erected by human beings.

Nanak's fantastic journey on earth is still very much alive today.

GLOSSARY

Adi Granth: the first book, the collection of poems put together in 1604.

Amrita, amrit: divine nectar, the elixir of immortality; the spiritual sentiment for the Adi Granth.

Arti: a form of Hindu worship.

Assura: demon.

Baba: father, title of respect given to saintly person.

Banjara: gypsy.

Bhagat, Bhakta: a Hindu mystic devoted to a personal God; a Hindu Sufi; saint.

Brahm bhoj: Hindu sacred meal.

Brahmin: member of the highest of the four Hindu castes; originally all Brahmins were priests.

Dargah: Muslim monastery; the presence of God.

Devas: gods.

Dharamsala: hostel that houses pilgrims.

Fakir: ascetic, hermit, yogi, sadhu.

Guru: spiritual master.

Hajj: Muslim pilgrimage to Mecca.

Hajji: Muslim pilgrim to Mecca.

Janamsakhi: account of the birth and life; biography.

Janeu: sacred cord worn by the upper caste Hindus.

Kaaba: Sacred black stone in Mecca, the focal point of the Hajj.

Khan: 'sovereign' in Turkish.

Kshatriya: Hindu warrior caste, second to Brahmin.

Langar: community kitchen.

Madrasa: Muslim school.

Maulavi: Muslim priest or wise man.

Nam: Divine name; the Word; *logos;* the spirit of God.

Namaz: ritual Muslim prayer performed five times a day.

Patti: Small wooden tablet.

Pir: Muslim spiritual leader of the Sufi order.

Punjab: land of five rivers in North India.

Punjabi: language of Punjab.

Pundit: Hindu priest.

Qazi: Muslim judge adept in Islamic law.

Raag (Raga): Array of melodic structures in Indian music.

Rebab: bowed instrument with one, two or three strings

Rupees: Indian currency.

Sadhu: ascetic, hermit, yogi and fakir.

Samadhi: state of meditation.

Sangam: confluence of rivers.

Sastra: old Hindu philosophic treatise.

Siddha: Yogi adept in occult powers.

Sufi: Muslim mystical thinker.

Sri Guru Granth Sahib Ji (Adi Granth): Sacred Book Guru Master; the name of the sacred book of the Sikhs given in 1708.

Vedas: Religious texts of Hindus written in Sanskrit beginning in the fifteenth century BC.

Yogi: Sadhu, ascetic, hermit, fakir.

ACKNOWLEDGMENTS

"Travelling Light – Legends of an Indian Fakir" was first written in French. Thanks to Marlyse Fleury (Geneva, Switzerland) for the initial reading and basic corrections to the French version, as well as for encouraging me to pursue the project. Geetanjali Kapoor of Bangalore, India, undertook the arduous work of illustrating the stories I cannot praise her enough for the frequent changes she had to make to satisfy my image of Nanak Dev as a rustic modern traveller and not a saintly person dressed like a sadhu, or a yogi, or a mullah. As she did not know French and not all the stories are available in English, I roughly translated them into English for her. This led to the idea of preparing the stories in English. Then comes my encounter with my English language editor, Robert Streit, whom I met again in the summer of 2018 after 55 years. I recall memories of my short stay with his wonderful loving family on Long Island, New York, in 1963, when Rob was still in high school. On learning that he is a retired editor, I could not resist asking him to edit these tales. Besides editing he gave me much practical advice in preparing the manuscript. Thank you, Rob. Finally I am indebted to W. John Rogers for editing and proofreading the text one last time and also making a donation to FFI rather than accept payment. ?

ABOUT THE AUTHOR

NAGINDER SINGH SEHMI graduated from Trinity College, Dublin University in 1963 where he studied history, geography, psychology and public administration. Then he obtained a postgraduate diploma in hydrology and water resources in Prague and served as hydrologist in the Kenya Ministry for Water and then in the World Meteorological Organization (WMO) for 27 years. From a young age he questioned the utility of religious traditions, especially in the Sikh community. In the light of his technical and scientific knowledge, he was convinced that most of the religious practices had seriously deviated from writings of the founders, in particular Nanak Dev, the first guru of the Sikhs. The only way Naginder could demonstrate this was to know and make known what Nanak has written in his 974 songs. By translating these songs into French, he has offered a suitable tool to the French-speaking community in general and to academic researchers, using a platform that he believes could guide the world towards a just path.

Publications:
Twisted Turban, 2013, Mereo Memoirs publishers, UK
Fate of Indra, 2018, Cinnamon Teal, Goa, India
Les Chansons de Nanak Dev (eBook) Cinnamon Teal, Goa, India
Chants de Nanak le Premier Sikh (PDF) - http://bigbangyoga.org/les-chants-de-nanak-dev/

Les Chanson de Nanak Dev, Kindle edition
https://www.amazon.com/Chansons-Nanak-Dev-French-ebook/dp/B07NGMSGXR

E-mail: nsehmi@bluewin.ch
Web: www.bigbangyoga.org